Gambling with Love

Kaye Spencer

Lasterday Stories, L.L.C.

Gambling with Love

Cover design – Kaye Spencer

Published by Lasterday Stories, LLC
www.lasterdaystories.com

ISBN: 978-8-9930823-2-5
LCCN: 2025924611

"The stars move still, time runs, the clock will strike..."

Dr. Faustus

Christopher Marlowe

Chapter One

April 10, 1883 – Pine Tree Buttes, Wyoming Territory

"I'm sorry, sir, there are no vacancies."

Deputy Federal Marshal Nick Foster heard the desk clerk, but the woman at the poker table in the adjoining room had his attention. Seeing Lainie again was like taking a right hook to the gut—took the wind right out of him. Given how elusive she'd been, catching up with her in this railroad town surprised him. She didn't often play penny-ante places. Likely as not, it was the snowstorm keeping her here.

He'd tracked her to Tombstone where she'd been running a faro table, but he'd missed her by a week, which turned out to be his ongoing luck ever since. He'd followed her gambling trail to San Francisco, on up to Reno, over to Idaho, back to Colorado, on into Texas, and always just days behind her.

Following a lead to Dodge City, the deputy told him she'd been there, and he'd only missed her by hours. She'd met up with an older woman and small child—boy, he thought—who'd been in town a couple of days. From a snippet of conversation he'd overheard in a restaurant, the deputy said Lainie was headed for a poker game in Denver, but she was going on to Chicago first. Lainie had left on a stage, and the woman and boy had gone east by train.

Nick spoke over his shoulder. "The woman playing cards. She come in alone?"

The clerk said, "Yes, sir. On the stage, early today. The storm's shut down the stage and the train."

Just as he'd thought. "What's her room number?"

"I can't give—"

"It's business." Nick faced the clerk, opened his duster, and pulled his vest aside, which revealed the badge pinned on his shirt. "And it's confidential."

Indecision colored the man's face an unhealthy shade of gray. Nick waited. In his experience, fear of what would happen for not cooperating with a lawman usually won out over integrity. The clerk cast a wary eye about, opened a drawer beneath the counter top, looked around again, and brought out a key that he slid across the surface to Nick.

"Up the stairs. Room six."

Nick pocketed the key. "Bath facilities here?"

The clerk jerked a nod toward the back. "Down the hallway. First door on the left."

"Any chance of getting some grub and coffee? Lots of coffee?"

"There's always coffee at the bar, but the kitchen next door closed a while ago."

Nick tossed him a Gold Eagle. "Will that cover it?"

The clerk caught the coin, glanced around again, and tucked the windfall into a pocket. "With some to spare."

"Keep it."

Stranded travelers and tobacco smoke filled the hotel lobby, but no one seemed to notice Nick as he crossed to the bar and ordered whiskey. With his hat pulled low over his brow, Winchester cradled in the crook of an elbow, and bulging saddlebags slung over his shoulder, he looked like any other saddle tramp passing through. He wanted to keep it that way. Attention would come on its own soon enough.

He downed his drink, refilled, then took the glass and moved to where he could watch the card game unnoticed. Warming with the whiskey, he relaxed. Four players sat at the table—three men and Lainie. Furniture blocked Nick's view of one of the men, but he wasn't curious enough right then to care. The other two he pegged as cowboys waiting out the storm and passing the time with a friendly game of poker. They weren't serious players. They were the type Lainie usually took pity on and made sure they left the table with a few dollars more than when they started.

Nick glanced at the Regulator clock—ten forty-five. Lainie never played much past midnight; he had plenty of time. In another hour, she'd ask the bartender to prepare hot water if she was in the mood for tea or to brew up a pot of coffee if she wasn't planning on retiring for a while. Tossing off the whiskey, he made his way to the bath room.

An hour later, bathed, shaved, and his belly full, he felt like a new man in a clean set of clothes. Nick returned to the bar and paid for another whiskey. Nursing it along, with his elbow resting on the bar top, he watched the game out of Lainie's line of sight. Just before midnight, he started for the stairs.

"Gentlemen, do any of you know the time?"

He stopped in mid-step, one foot on the bottom stair, and stared straight ahead. The languid cadence of her cotton-soft southern drawl wafted in the air, embracing him with bitter-sweet memories of their last night together and the ring he hadn't put on her finger. The siren call in her voice tugged at his heart. Damn, he'd missed her, and now that he'd found her, his willpower to separate love from duty was quickly deteriorating into a one-sided, losing battle.

Someone reported the time. Chair legs scraped and boots shuffled on the hardwood floor.

"Gentlemen, this has been a lovely evening, but I must take my leave. I cannot go without my beauty rest."

Nick shifted his position. The two cowboys stood with hats in hand, uttering their thanks for the game, but the third man remained seated. Nick got a good look at him. His face wasn't familiar, but his type was. Cardsharp. The sort who came to the table with genteel larceny in mind, ready to fleece unsuspecting lambs foolish enough to play the master in his own game. The jeweled stickpin in his lapel and ostentatious diamond ring on a little finger smacked of extravagance and excess.

The man's manner was as controlled and cool as his black suit was expensive and tailored. His long, slender hands and nimble fingers bore the trademark of a professional gambler, and the cards fairly sang as he shuffled them. On sheer principle, Nick didn't like him. His kind were users and takers.

"It's still early, Lainie. Let me buy you a drink. Or coffee."

"Mrs. Conrad to you. You know full well after a game I take coffee or tea in my room alone, and I rarely drink alcohol except on very special occasions. Stranded in this quaint little cow town does not qualify as a commemorative event."

He continued deftly manipulating the cards. "You're right. I do know that about you, Mrs. Conrad." Then the corners of his lips turned up in a sly smile. "I assume you'll be in Denver this weekend. We should make plans to celebrate after I win the tournament."

The fiery spark in Lainie's eyes was the only outward indication the man had ruffled her impassive composure.

"Yes, I will be a player in that game, and it will be my pleasure to finally take all of your money. Perhaps I'll feel generous after I win to front you a little something so you can leave town." Lainie nodded to the cowboys. "Again. Gentlemen, goodnight."

With the fluid movement of a striking snake, the cardsharp snatched hold of Lainie's hand and halted her exit. She neither struggled nor spoke a word. To anyone who didn't know her, she might have seemed indifferent, but Nick recognized the unreserved loathing in the steady, steely gaze she fixed upon the gambler's face. There was a history between them that Nick wanted to know more about.

"Stay awhile, Mrs. Conrad. We've known each other long enough to put aside formal pretenses. Let's dispense with this ongoing façade. It's tiresome. There's no reason for either of us to spend the rest of this night, or any night in the future, alone." The gambler raked his gaze over Lainie's body, his lips curled in a leer that said he was a man accustomed to getting what he wanted.

Nick's temper rose, but he held back, watching. If he knew nothing else about Lainie Conrad, he knew she was capable of handling herself with any man in any situation. Still, he pushed back the side of his duster and flipped the leather thong off the hammer of the short-barreled .44 at his hip.

Both cowboys voiced their disapproval of the gambler's insinuation, but Lainie waved the well-meaning young men into silence. "Good night, Mr. Tolliver." The snowstorm held more warmth than her tone.

Tolliver was a name Nick had heard during his search in the gambling towns for Lainie, but never linked with her name. He made a mental note to check into Tolliver's past tomorrow, but for the next few hours, Lainie was all he was interested in.

Taking the stairs to the second-floor hallway, Nick let himself into Lainie's room. Low light glowed from the oil lamp on the bedside table, and fire burned in the parlor stove near the bed, neither of which surprised him. Lainie liked to be comfortable, and paying to have a warm, lighted room awaiting her arrival was something she would do.

Stowing his gear and coat in a corner, he looked the room over. Apparently, she was traveling light nowadays. Her steamer trunks and portmanteau were missing. It looked like she was living out of a couple of oversized leather bags. For as fastidious in her dress and grooming as she was, that wasn't like her, which made him wonder what she was up to.

Nick added another piece of wood and a shovelful of coal to the stove, grateful to be inside after riding three hours through the raging blue norther that, right now, was doing its damnedest to batter down the building with gusts of howling wind that rattled windowpanes and slammed loose shutters. He looped his gun belt over a bedpost within easy grasp, stretched out on the bed, situated his hat on the off-hand side, and slipped a set of handcuffs beneath it. He'd give her a chance to come with him of her own accord, but knowing Lainie... Well, she wasn't getting away so easily this time.

While he waited, it felt good to let the weariness of the trail ease from his bones. Minutes later, the doorknob grated, and the door opened. That she didn't use her key told him she knew he was waiting for her. It was her gambler's nature; she noticed every little detail.

She paused at the threshold, coffee pot in hand, and the trim line of her figure silhouetted for a moment against the dim yellow hallway light before she stepped into the room, closed and locked the door. Crossing the few steps to the stove, she situated the coffee pot on the flat top, and placed a coffee cup, the room key, along with her reticule, on the table. Taking her time, and seemingly oblivious to his presence, she removed her short-waisted jacket, draped it over a chair back, and sashayed to the bed.

Lamp light shadows played off her swept-up golden tresses, and visions of their last night together in New Orleans seized him. Right then, he hated himself for how shamelessly he still loved her.

"You can only imagine my extreme disappointment when I saw you standing on the stairs. All this time I'd hoped you were dead."

The teasing welcome in her tone belied her harsh words, and a warm rush of missing her made it hard to keep a clear head with a churning den of rattlers twisting around in his belly. He'd never loved a woman before Lainie waltzed into his life, and even though she'd run out on him almost as quickly as she'd arrived, there was no room in his heart for another woman. There never would be.

"Your aim was off. It was just a graze, but it rang my bell and bled like hell." There wasn't enough light for her to see it, but he turned his head and pointed to the scar that began at his right temple and ended over his ear.

"Why are you assuming my aim was off? By your own admission, it did knock you out, which was the object of my intent, I'll have you know."

Nick cocked an eyebrow, mocking her. "So, you're a sharp-shooter?"

He loved the lyrical lilt of her laughter, and she laughed now.

"Next time you use that little parlor gun of yours, make sure you're close enough to cram it right into the poor chump's belly when you pull the trigger. You still might not kill him, but you'll increase your chances of slowing him down, that's for sure."

"Why, thank you so much for the advice. However, in my defense, if you hadn't tried to disarm me, I wouldn't have pulled the trigger. It was your own fault that I shot you. Your ultimatum left me no choice, but to demonstrate the sincerity of my convictions." Her voice dripped of syrupy sweet sarcasm.

Nick remembered all too well. "Are you planning on shooting me again?"

A grin played at the corners of her lips. "That depends upon your intentions toward my virtue." Lainie busied herself with adjusting the lamp wick until she was satisfied with the glow.

Her subtle jasmine fragrance made it difficult to keep his hands to himself. "You know my intentions toward your virtue have never been honorable." Self-constraint vanished. Pulling her down to sit beside him, he drew her skirt along her legs a handful of cloth at a time. Inching his hand between her knees, he stroked along her silky-smooth thigh just to see where they stood with each other. Although her eyes held a devilish gleam that promised heaven at the end of his journey, neither did she encourage further exploration. It was a reminder that if a romantic dalliance was in the offing, it would be on her terms, and he withdrew his hand.

"What was the real reason you shot me?"

For an instant, a shadow of regret—or, maybe sorrow—dulled the luster in her blue eyes.

"Does it matter? It's only important for you to know I only shoot when I've exhausted all other options."

"How many people have you shot?"

"So far?" Leaning down, she murmured against his lips, "Just you, darlin'. Just you."

Her breath, sweet with peppermint, sent a rush of pent-up, fiery need for her pulsing through his body like lava flowing down a mountain side. He savored her mouth, losing himself in memories of their brief, but intense weeks together.

She whispered in his ear, "I've missed you, darlin'. Have you missed me?"

"You crossed my mind a time or two." Shit. He'd thought of little else. The mixture of lust and love tinged with a good dose of broken heart clawed at his belly. A moaning sigh rose from her throat as she slipped a leg over him, molding her body prone onto his. He wanted her to stay in his arms like this forever, but knew with a deep aching in his heart that it wasn't likely to be the way this was going to end.

Lainie sat up, straddled his groin, and idly fiddled with his vest buttons. He recalled the magic touch in those fingers, soft and tender against his skin. Flicking open the pearl button at the V of her blouse, he paused to see if she would stop him. Her hint of a smirk encouraged him, and he went down the line of buttons until her blouse gaped open. It would be nothing at all to lift the veil of her chemise and free her from the constraints of her corset, but the loneliness he'd learned to live with since the last time they'd made love came rushing back. He wanted to forgive her for running out on him; he almost had...until this moment.

Almost.

"I heard you were dealing faro in Tombstone."

"It was as temporary as it was necessary at the time. You know faro isn't my game. I'm a five-card-draw girl."

"Then you moved on to San Francisco and up to Reno—"

"Have you been following me?" She tilted her head.

"Yeah. There's trouble brewing. We need to talk about it."

"I'm a gambler, darlin'. I live on the edge of trouble."

Lainie's breath was warm and moist against his neck, and he melted into the pillow, closing his eyes to her feathery kisses caressing his skin, wanting nothing more than to give himself over to pleasure, but duty brought him back. Sitting up, he encircled her waist with his arms. She mistook his intent and slipped her arms around his neck, pressing her breasts against his chest as she lifted her face to kiss him.

He spoke as her lips touched his. "I heard you took a local kid for a couple of thousand dollars. I don't want to believe it. That's not the way you play."

Lainie leaned back. "So searching for me wasn't just because you missed me?" She huffed out a put-on, disappointed sigh. "I think that hurts my feelings."

"Lainie, this is important. Tell me what happened in Charlotte."

Her hesitation told him she was considering how much to say, if anything.

"Very well. That kid had a name—Dean Saunderson—and he was at least twenty-one, if he was a day. He lamentably fancied himself a gambler. I simply demonstrated an important life lesson and put him out of the game before he wagered a goodly portion of his family's property that, I'm quite certain, he had no legal rights to."

"That's not all of it, Lainie."

She arched a curious eyebrow. "Oh? Please, do go on."

There was no way to soften what he had to say, so he laid it out straight. "That boy died, Lainie."

Chapter Two

Lainie didn't respond for some moments. "Yes, I know. I read about his death in a newspaper. Such a tragic end for one so young."

"Is that all you know about it?"

Suspicion flittered across her face. "Why do you ask?"

"After the game, witnesses saw you go into his room."

"How do you know this, and why does it matter?"

"There are some stories going around, and it matters, because I'm worried about you."

"Stories? As in rumors? Well, what people say about me is of no concern of mine. Why are you worried?"

Exasperated, Nick said, "Stop answering my questions with questions. Just tell me what happened that night."

"First, tell me why you care what happened."

The warning in her eyes said he'd pressed too hard, too fast, and she was an uncooperative decision away from refusing to talk about this.

"Take it easy. I want to know so I can help you if anything comes of—" He started over. "There are rumors of an investigation into his death."

"And there is an insinuation in that statement."

Nick blew out a tired breath. "Just tell me, Lainie."

"There isn't much to tell. I had spent a delightful evening playing poker with several gentlemen at the hotel. As the night went on, Dean's whiskey consumption increased in direct proportion to his inability to play a decent game. I simply played in such a manner as to put him out of the game before another player took advantage of his inexperience."

Nick frowned, trying to interpret her meaning. "You're saying you played fair and square, but someone in the game was cheating?"

With put-on offense, she playfully slapped his chest. "Nick Foster, I always play an honest game. The day I resort to cheating to win is the day I give up playing poker for a living. And, yes, someone was cheating. Dean wasn't a good enough player sober, let alone drunk, to recognize a bottom deal."

He could believe she'd do that. "Go on."

"Apparently, after I left the game, someone filled his head with nonsense about what I owed him. With the whiskey giving him courage, he came to my room, pounding upon my door and shouting that I give over of certain favors as consolation for his monetary loss and the damage done to his pride in front of the other gentlemen. I certainly couldn't have him in my room, so I convinced him we should discuss this in his room."

"That doesn't make sense. Why didn't you stay locked inside your room and let hotel staff handle him?"

"Because I felt sorry for him. Nick, he was a sweet young man, in over his head gambling—and entirely too inebriated to be a danger to anyone but himself. He was like a little lost pup and in no condition to be left alone, so I stayed with him, holding his hand while he babbled on about his deepest troubles."

He wanted to believe what she said, but it wasn't up to him to determine her innocence or guilt. His job was to bring her in. "And that was it? You smoothed his ruffled feathers, tucked him in bed, and went on your way."

Lainie looked at him many long moments. "Yes. It was such a shame his life was so complicated for his young age."

"There was a tea cup on the table beside his bed."

"That is your second insinuation."

"Explain it."

"I was preparing to have tea when Dean came to my room, so I took the tray with tea pot and two cups with me. I left a cup for him, and brought the tray with me when I returned to my room."

"Did you put something in his?"

She didn't answer, and he knew.

"What did you put in it?"

"Nick, he was inconsolable. I had to do something to help him."

"Lainie, stop being so evasive and just tell me."

"I carry a rather potent sleeping draught for the occasional times when insomnia troubles me. I put a few drops into his tea."

"Is that all?"

"More insinuations?"

Nick raised his eyebrows.

Lainie exhaled, clearly impatient with his questioning. "I also prepared an old family remedy for sleeping—absinthe and bourbon."

Nick raked his fingers through his hair. "Good God almighty, Lainie. Absinthe on top of what he'd already been drinking. The green fairy probably scared him to death."

"I prepared it. I didn't say he drank it." Indignant, Lainie slapped her hands on her hips. "I am a firm believer that if a man can't hold his liquor, then he shouldn't drink at all. There's no telling what he might do. Why, it's just embarrassing to his manly dignity."

"Whoa." Nick eyed her. "He didn't drink it?"

"No. Not while I was there. Once I sat beside him and held his hand while he talked, he calmed himself."

"What if he drank it all later?"

"If you mean, would it have killed him... No. I had put so few sleeping drops in the tea that a few yawns would have been the result. It takes much, much more than I used to put a big strapping boy of his size into a deep sleep. My intent was simply to calm his amorous and rather clumsy attempts at affection."

"What troubles did he have?"

"He was caught in a terrible ordeal between his parents and his lover." Lainie stared across the room with a faraway memory soft in her eyes. "He just wanted to be happy, and his family couldn't accept it." She looked back at Nick. "I stayed with him until he fell asleep. He was alive when I left."

"And that was it?"

"Yes. And that was it."

Nick considered which direction to take his questioning. "Back in New Orleans, you said your last name was Dorsett. Why didn't you tell me you were married?"

"Recently widowed. There's a difference. Dorsett is my mother's maiden name and my middle name. Sometimes a girl just needs her privacy."

"You told me you were in town on business."

"Yes. My husband had won the deed to a house and several acres some months before he died. I had returned to sell it, but a situation arose that prevented me from finalizing the sale."

"And that coincided with our abrupt goodbye?"

Lainie smiled at his choice of words. "In fact, it did."

"Where did you go?"

"Where do you suppose? I went gambling." She leaned low over his chest. "Must we continue talking about all of this? I am seriously beginning to lose my ardor, and that would be such a shame, considering how long it's been since I've had your more than adequate manhood at my disposal."

Damn it felt good to be with her; he couldn't help himself. Not so long ago he'd sworn he never wanted to see her again, but she'd stayed in his head and in his heart. And now that they were together again, he couldn't keep lying to himself that he'd only gone after her to prevent another man from bringing her in for the bounty. Lainie was his woman, and he'd do anything to have her back. Much as he wanted to pursue what she clearly had on her mind, he couldn't do it.

On a hard exhale, he said, "You're a wanted woman, Lainie."

He'd expected a reaction from her, but not the one she gave, which was a smile that told him she didn't care.

"I suspected this is where this interrogation was going. Why didn't you just say so to begin with? And to think that in your dedication you've ridden through a snowstorm just to tell me. I think you really do love me."

Her mocking riled him. "I want to talk to you about that, too, but there's something more important right now." Nick removed a folded paper from his vest pocket. "This handbill's set to circulate in a couple of weeks."

Lainie unfolded the paper and read aloud. "'Wanted for Murder. Lainie Conrad. Also goes by the names Elaine Dorsett, Lainie Dorsett, and Mrs. Seaton Conrad. Frequents gambling halls, saloons, and finer gambling establishments. Blonde hair. Blue eyes. Good figure. Tall. In late twenties to early thirties. Travels alone.'"

A splotch of pink darkened her cheeks. "Well, I do declare. Such bad taste to allude to a lady's age." She tossed the handbill aside. "I can't bother with this right now. I have an important engagement in a few days. I will deal with it at a later time."

"You can't ignore this." Neither could he. There weren't many days left of the grace period he'd negotiated for finding her himself before the handbill went out. He'd cut the bounty information off the bottom of the paper, so she wouldn't know there was a price on her head. He couldn't do that to her right then. It was too harsh. He'd tell her if there was no other way to get her cooperation.

"I can if I want." Lainie rolled her palms up and down his biceps and over his shoulders, then leaned low and placed a line of butterfly-soft kisses on his neck. "Let me show you how easy it is to put troublesome thoughts aside." She whispered against his skin, "Really, Nick. Why are you here? How do you know about the handbill? And don't lie to me."

Placing her hands flat on his chest, she massaged her fingers against his shirt in little circles that widened with each caress, teasing at the placard of front buttons. "Let's not— What is this?" Yanking his vest opened, she stared at his shirt. "When did you become a U.S. Marshal?" With a tentative touch, she traced the badge with her fingertips.

"Deputy Marshal. I was a lawman when we met."

"Apparently a dishonest lawman. Do you always hide your badge?"

"Pinning it on the outside sometimes makes for a good target."

"In New Orleans... You said you were part of a trial, but you were so close-mouthed. I assumed you were a juror or a witness, which is why I didn't press for details. You could have told me."

"Well, I'll tell you now. The defendant was under federal arrest. There were four deputy marshals assigned to escort him between the jail and courthouse and to sit behind him in court and to make sure his cronies didn't try to spring him. We worked in pairs. A. J. took more of his share of my night watches so you and I could have the evenings together that we did."

Warm remembrance softened her features. "I knew there was a soft heart inside that gruff old man."

"He wouldn't like being called old man. He's still got an eye for the ladies. Hell, he's as spry as—"

"As what? As spry in bed as you are? Maybe I should find out for myself."

This was the light-hearted, spirited Lainie he remembered, and missed. "Yeah, well, don't be too careless with your teasing. He's liable to take you up on your offer. He was sweet on you from that first night we all had dinner together." With A. J. in the conversation, duty once again returned to the forefront.

"I'm taking you back to Charlotte." He slipped his left hand under his hat.

"Nick, you haven't been listening. I'm leaving on the next westbound train or stagecoach."

"That sounds like a refusal to cooperate with a lawman."

"Am I under arrest?"

"Yeah. You are." He grabbed her right arm, slapped an end of the handcuffs around her wrist then hooked the other end around his left wrist, all the while bracing for her attack.

"What—"

Her moment of wide-eyed disbelief dissolved into a mischievous grin that made him nervous as hell. She'd looked at him the same way in New Orleans just before she'd pulled her derringer on him. A warning went off in his head to check her for weapons, but right then she bent down and breathed warm, wet kisses onto the hollow below his ear.

He sucked in a ragged breath, barely managing to get the words out. "You're taking this better than I expected."

She mumbled an endearment against his lips then tugged his shirttail free of his trousers and worked her kisses and caressing fingers low across his belly. So help him, he didn't want her to stop. He turned himself over to her touch, her mouth, her caresses. Her exploring fingers went downward, undid his trousers, and dipped low inside the waistband. His belly tightened; his need for her surged with the satiny warmth of her fingers teasing him.

On a rasping moan, he warned, "That's about all I can take of that before we get down to something more serious." Through the sensual haze she'd drawn over his will-power, a remnant of responsibility forced its way through, and he groaned out dutiful, memorized words. "By federal warrant...Lainie...Conrad...You're under arrest...for suspicion of murder—"

"Shh." She placed silencing fingertips on his lips. "I do love a man dedicated to his job but, darlin', this isn't the time."

She arranged her skirts out of the way, and settled over him, the bare skin of her thighs warm and snug against his body. Closing his eyes, he put his hands on her hips and held her to him, more than ready to pursue where this was rapidly going, just like it had been back on those hot, lazy Louisiana nights—

Cold, hard metal pressed against his belly, and he didn't have to open his eyes to know what it was. "There's nothing quite like a gun shoved in your gut to kill the ardor."

"Is this point-blank enough this time?" The husky tone in her voice carried a harsh finality.

He wasn't surprised to see the two-shot .41 caliber over-under Remington derringer Lainie gripped in her hand. Slowly, he lifted his gaze to her face.

Her eyes were narrow slits of fury; her jaw was set in hard anger. He'd seen both the expression and the gun before, and this was shaping up to be a similarly unpleasant experience.

"Now, just bring out that little ol' key, undo these handcuffs, and I'll still love you when I leave here."

An apologetic grin twitched his mouth, and he shook his head. "Sorry, Lainie. Apparently, you weren't listening, either.

I said you're under arrest, and I'm taking you back to Charlotte to face charges."

Her eyes flashed with a dark, wicked gleam. "Nick," she cooed as she pressed the derringer just a little harder into his belly. "You know I'll pull the trigger, and where will that get us? You'll be bleeding. I'll go through your pockets for the key and then leave you here all alone. We won't be friends anymore."

There was no bluff in her voice. She'd shot him once, and Nick knew she'd do it again. And this time she was close enough for her little parlor gun to do serious damage. "Lainie... You need to know—" He cupped her neck with his free hand and drew her down as he half-raised up to meet her. "I don't have the key on me." Slamming his mouth on hers, he forced his tongue between her lips, and kissed her like he'd never get the chance again.

Her regretful moan was his only warning.

Chapter Three

Nick twisted his body and slapped Lainie's hand at the instant she pulled the trigger, which deflected the barrel enough that she only got off one shot and the bullet burned a gouge along his hip bone before the derringer went skittering across the hardwood floor.

Bolting upright, he grabbed his side. "Damn it, Lainie! What the hell's wrong with you?"

"You told me to hold it right against your belly. Don't blame me for your poor advice."

"Why are you so hell-bent on killing me?"

"Oh, stop your whining. I had no more intention of killing you this time than last time. If you wouldn't persist on getting in the way when I need to leave, we wouldn't have these little lover's spats."

"Spats? I'm getting damn tired of the way you say goodbye." Lifting his hand from the wound, he looked at the raw gash and the blood running down his side. "Shit. Shit! Get me something to put on this." He clamped his hand against the wound.

"Just how am I supposed to do that? I am somewhat hampered in my movements by your clever little trick to keep me close to you." Lainie yanked their bound arms with a violence that sent Nick into another round of cussing at the sharp stab of pain her movement caused.

He left the bed in a bound, which dumped her onto the mattress in an unladylike bounce. "I hope like hell the storm covered the sound of your little popgun. I'm the only lawman we need involved in this..." He threw her a frowning glance. "...tiff."

"It will serve you right if you have to explain why you were taking advantage of a helpless prisoner."

"That's a laugh. There's nothing helpless about you." Setting his sights on the washbasin and pitcher, he dragged Lainie unceremoniously off the bed as he strode across the room, disregarding the uncomplimentary names issuing from her mouth as she stumbled at his heels.

Jerking her up beside him, he ordered, "Get that towel wet and wring it out good then hold it here." He turned his bloody side toward her, but Lainie ignored him in her preoccupation of buttoning herself back into her clothing.

"Damnit, Lainie—"

"Do not bark orders at me. I'm your prisoner, not your nursemaid or your personal servant. You brought this on yourself. What did you expect when you handcuffed me?"

"I expected you to go peacefully—"

"I have no intention of going anywhere peacefully or...or...unpeacefully with you. This storm has already delayed my schedule. I am so thankful I've already sent my luggage on ahead, so I don't have to deal with it in this frightful weather." She absently patted her hair into place.

"I'm bleeding here. I don't give a damn about your luggage."

"Well, you should. I have an important engagement at the end of the week, and I must look my best."

"Yeah," he said through gritted teeth. "I heard you mention your important engagement downstairs." Pouring water into the basin, he dipped a corner of the hand towel into the water, and sucked in a raspy breath when he pressed the wet, cold cloth against his skin. "Right now, your poker game and your wardrobe aren't my main concerns." He cut her an impatient glare, and she made an ugly face in return.

"I have already put up the thirty-thousand-dollar entry fee, and I will forfeit that money if I do not arrive on time which, I assure you, Marshal Foster, will not happen."

Nick stared at her, his mind not comprehending. Finally, he stammered, "Thiry... Thirty thousand dollars? You have that much ready cash?"

"More." She shrugged offhandedly. "Much, much more."

"Then losing a little pocket-money won't put you in a bind." He meant every bit of the sarcasm in his tone.

Lainie bristled; her eyes flashed with affronted pride. "I never play unless I can afford to lose, but I will not miss the game." She shook her cuffed wrist in his face. "This is unacceptable."

"Damn it, stop yanking my arm. That hurts."

"Your little scratch is not my problem."

"Scratch? That bullet could have gone through my lung or kidney—"

"But it didn't. Don't be such a baby. I wasn't aiming for your vital organs. You'll live."

Through clenched teeth, and out of patience, he warned, "You are going back to Charlotte."

"I most certainly am not." Wheeling, she took off toward the bed, pulling him along with her.

"What the hell are you doing? This is not the time for a roll in the hay."

"Don't flatter yourself, Marshal. I am not interested in playing any more parlor games with you."

Almost too late, he realized she was going for his gun. He stopped dead in his tracks and spun her around. "Oh, no, you don't, sweetheart." Jerking her to him, he snaked his arms around her waist, his handcuffed arm bending her arm back at an awkward angle behind her.

She fought like a Kilkenny cat to free herself from the steel bands of his arms around her body amid an outburst of cursing without, he noticed, repeating a single word.

"Such language from a lady. I should wash your mouth out with soap." The more she struggled, the more he laughed. She was the feistiest woman he'd ever known, in or out of bed, and her fiery passion made him love her even more.

When she shifted her body, he felt her knee coming toward his groin, and he turned his hip into her just in time to deflect the well-placed blow and wrenched her handcuffed arm to drive home his control over her. She gasped, almost cried out, at the stabbing pain shooting across her shoulder blades, but she still threw herself backward and dragged them down to the mattress.

"Lainie! Stop fighting me. It was either me or a stranger—a stranger who might have more on his mind than just bringing you in. That's why I didn't just go on to Denver back when I was in Dodge and heard that's where you were headed. I could have waited for you to show up there and saved myself all this time chasing you around the country." He loosened his hold. "But I was afraid someone would get to you first."

Flat on her back and pinned under him, Nick looked into the angriest pair of blue eyes he'd ever seen. There was payback in that dark glare, too, and no mistaking her wish for his demise. But at least she'd stopped struggling. Damn, but she was as wickedly enticing right then as he'd ever seen her, and he'd have kissed her, but he remembered it was just that kind of activity that had gotten him shot...twice.

He had one consolation. As long as she stayed mad, it kept his fine-line between lawman and lover as a solid barrier he wouldn't be tempted to cross. Unless she cried. He'd always been a sucker for a crying woman.

Then, there it was—a misty shine of betrayal brimming in her eyes. He set his jaw against the aching in his heart but, thankfully, she blinked away the emotion before it took hold of either of them. Nick couldn't decide if she was throwing out a threat or a dare. Either way, a little warning went off in his head that she was conceding defeat too easily. Still, he let it go in his relief that she was cooperating and not crying

"You can let me up. I won't fight any more."

Tentatively, not quite trusting her, he loosened his hold, tested her reaction, and then rolled off of her to sit on the edge of the bed. Lainie sat up, but didn't look at him.

"Give me your word you'll behave yourself, and I'll take off the handcuffs. We can stay right here until the next eastbound train comes through."

Lainie lifted her chin, her dignity returned. "You know as well as I, that at my first opportunity, I will escape, so it would be an outright lie if I made that promise. It would distress me to be the reason your reputation and good name are questioned at some future time, so it is best if you take me to the jail until the train arrives."

Exasperated that her words belied the haughty gleam in her eyes and her saucy smirk that promised you won't win this battle, Nick said, "Damn it, Lainie. I don't understand how you can say you love me, yet you're so damned determined to get away from me."

"You complicate my life at the most inconvenient times. You're too much in love with a woman who can't give you what you want."

That came out of nowhere, and it set him back. "What do I want?"

The angry edge to her features softened. "A place where your wanderings can bring you home at night instead of living hotel room to hotel room, or sleeping on the trail by a lonely campfire."

She knew him well. That was exactly what he wanted. "There's a wanderlust inside you, too, that's more than where gambling takes you. In a way, we're alike in our nomadic lives. Do you gamble because you can't make a living any other way? You said you have plenty of money, so why not quit gambling and do something else?"

"What do you suggest?"

Shrugging, he said, "You could marry a lawman, and we could build a home—a nice little home in a meadow, where we could run a few head of cows and horses."

"Nick, I'm a gambler, because I love the life. I love the excitement of the game, of challenging myself against an opponent, and knowing I'm good at what I do. No—that's not quite true. I'm one of the best there is." She took a deep breath, held it, and then exhaled slowly. "Even if I didn't love the gambling life, I have to finish..." She shook her head.

"What's going on with you? Give me something I can understand."

Lainie's shoulders fell on a sorrowful sigh. "My husband was murdered. There are unresolved issues of which I must bring to conclusion."

"Oh, hell, Lainie." Nick whistled between his teeth. "Murder. Well, I know something about that. It leaves an empty aching inside that never goes away."

"Yes, it does," she whispered.

This put a new light on things. "I'm sorry about your husband. It doesn't matter how you lose someone you love, it twists a person up inside, makes it hard to keep a level head when you're drowning in grief and regrets. My only brother was murdered."

Lainie's head came up. Sorrow and compassion puckered her brow. "I'm so sorry. How did it happen?"

"Stagecoach hold-up. He was gunned down protecting an elderly woman. He left behind a wife and two young kids." In his mind, he was a scared seventeen-year-old kid again, looking down at his brother's body where he lay on that lonely stage road north of San Antonio. "I memorized the face of each one of the bandits, swearing that someday, somehow I'd make them pay for what they'd done.

"You avenged your brother's death?"

Nick nodded. "It took me three years, but I found them all. Every bounty I collected, I gave to his widow. Then I became a lawman."

"Afterward... Did it help make the pain of his loss bearable?"

Shrugging, he said, "Maybe. Sometimes. Each day gets easier to let go of a little more bitterness, a little more of the guilt for not being able to stop it from happening."

"Then perhaps you can understand something of what drives me."

"Lainie. I have to know. What we had in New Orleans...were you just passing the time with me?"

Her sigh held the shaky threat of tears all wrapped up with exhaustion, sorrow, and a longing for something deeper he couldn't put words to, but that he also felt down deep inside.

"I hadn't thought I could love again after Seaton died. It was too soon. Then, I met you..." Blinking tears, she looked away. "What I feel for you isn't the same as what I felt for Seaton, but it is every bit as real and as strong." She looked at him. "Perhaps even stronger, if that's possible."

Her confession surprised him, touched him.

"I was afraid if I let myself love you, I'd never finish what I had to do for the sake of my—" A hiccupping sob got in the way, and it took her several moments to regain composure. Tossing her head, she defied her memories and her pain. "Over his grave, I vowed to Seaton that his death would not go unavenged. I will not renege on that promise."

"Why didn't you just tell me? I could have—would have—helped you. I still will. We can do this together."

"Because if I'd shared that with you, I was afraid I'd lose my will to continue. It would have been so easy to forget the pain and give you my heart, but it wouldn't have been fair to you. Until this is over—until I've achieved what I'm after—I cannot give myself wholly to you." She touched his face, and he put his hand over hers to hold her hand against his skin. After a few seconds, she let her hand drop to her side.

"You are the kind of man who loves once in a lifetime. Seaton was cut from the same cloth. My future was—is—uncertain." She paused, her gaze searching his. "The night before we parted in New Orleans, two things happened. There was a chance encounter in the hotel lobby...an observation. A fleeting instant of understanding. Where I thought my life was going took a different path in those moments."

"The path you're on now?"

"Yes."

"And you can't tell me about it?"

"No. I can't."

Nick nodded, not in understanding or even sympathy, but to himself as he tried to make some sort of sense of her words. "You said two things happened. What was the other?

"I found the ring in your coat pocket."

Nick swallowed hard, afraid to ask, but unable not to. "Would you have accepted?"

Her eyes misted, and she nodded. "Yes, but because of what I'd witnessed a few minutes before in the lobby, I had no choice but to break your heart, maybe even make you hate me, so you could go on with your life and forget me."

He ran his hand over his face as he blew out a ragged breath. "It didn't work."

"I know," she whispered. "Everything I wanted was all wrapped up in you. It still is. When I think of you, I see a husband. A home. A father for our children..." Fighting back tears took her voice.

He couldn't stay mad at her. How could he, when all he wanted to do was hold her, tell her that somehow this would all work out all right? But he couldn't. He was a lawman first, and there was nothing he could do to help her with whatever it was that was tormenting her, at least not until the Charlotte mess was cleaned up. From the look in her eyes, she knew it, too.

"Until this part of my life is resolved, I can't be completely yours. You deserve more than a few shattered pieces of my heart." Taking a deep breath, she set her shoulders, and looked him square in the eyes. "Let's get on with this. It's time to go."

He hated that she was right. For both their sakes, she had to stay locked up until they left town. He was practically helpless to resist her feminine wiles, and she knew it all too well, but damn if he didn't feel like a lowdown heel.

Nick helped her gather her belongings, retrieved the derringer from the floor, and stuffed it into his pocket. Then he dug out the handcuff key from his saddlebags, removed the end locked around his arm, put on his coat, and then closed the end of the handcuff around his wrist again. He draped her hooded, woolen cloak around her shoulders and helped her wrap her knitted scarf around her neck. She waited with cold detachment while he slung his gun belt around his hips and crammed his hat on his head.

Without talking, they made their way along the dimly lit hallway to the stairway and down to the gloomy lobby that was as empty as his heart as they passed through on their way out into the snowy night.

There were times when he didn't like this job, and damned if this wasn't one of them.

Chapter Four

Hunkered into his coat, Nick made his way along the early morning, snow-covered street to the telegraph office. A friendly telegraph operator greeted him, although his gaze lingered on the badge pinned to the outside of Nick's coat.

"I need to send two telegrams. Are the wires up?"

"Yes. Working just fine." The man took the paper with Nick's handwritten messages.

"What's the status on the trains?"

"The railroad is closed around Laramie from drifts and broken rails, which is not unusual in these spring snowstorms. Trains are routing in a loop through Denver down to the Kansas Pacific line going east. Probably better count on the westbounds coming through at night for the next couple of days before the schedule straightens back out to the regular morning run."

Nick thanked him for the information, stepped outside, and bumped into a woman carrying two cloth-covered picnic baskets, a pillow, and a woolen blanket. Tipping his hat, he said, "Pardon me, ma'am."

The woman scrutinized his badge. "Hmm. Are you headed for the sheriff's office?"

"Yes."

"Well, then, you can open the door when we get there." She thrust the larger basket into his hands. "I'm Maudie Wallace, the sheriff's wife."

"Nick Foster, Deputy U.S. Marshal."

"I suppose you're the marshal who arrested the danger ous criminal last night." Her disapproval was as chilly as the morning air. "I heard you barged right into her room, handcuffed her, and forced her to walk all the way from the hotel to the jail in the storm. *Hmmpf.* Didn't even let the poor girl get a decent night's sleep.

Amusing himself, he was tempted to describe what he and Lainie had really been doing when he arrested her. "She's wanted for suspicion of murder, ma'am."

Mrs. Wallace turned a disdainful eye on him. "So she explained. I told her I hoped if she had killed a man, that he had been her unfaithful lover, and she'd caught him with another woman. That's not murder. That's justice in my book."

Nick chuckled at how serious she was in her opinion. "Just how did you find out there was a prisoner, and when did you talk to her?"

"Hollis—you met him when you brought Miss Lainie in—is my husband's nephew, and he lives with us. He told me when he came home from his shift, so I came right over to ask if there was anything I could bring to make her more comfortable when I came back with breakfast."

"Breakfast?"

"I cook for the jailers and the prisoners."

He'd grown up in a small Texas town, so the speed at which gossip and news traveled, depending upon who was spreading it, didn't surprise him. Mrs. Wallace talked nonstop all the way to the jailhouse, and he listened with polite endurance.

"'Morning, Maudie." A gray-haired, grizzle-featured man greeted her from where he sat behind a desk. "Got a telegram from your husband this mornin'. Says he's on his way back from Dodge. Be here in a couple of days."

"Good morning, Layton. That is good to hear." Mrs. Wallace went on through the doorway in the center of the thick adobe and wood wall that separated the office from the two cells in the back. Over her shoulder, she said, "Marshal, the basket you're carrying is for Layton. Just leave it on the desk."

Layton grabbed the ring of keys from where they hung on a nail and followed her into the back. Nick heard the cell door open, and a few seconds later, it closed and locked. Layton returned to the desk, but Mrs. Wallace remained with Lainie.

Layton jerked a thumb toward the back. "So you're the one who brought Miss Lainie in last night."

Nick heard the same kind of disapproval in his voice that he'd heard in Mrs. Wallace's. He almost chuckled aloud. Lainie had a way of charming everyone she met, but they didn't know her like he did.

"I've been trailing her. She's a suspect in a North Carolina murder." Nick made it a habit to give out just enough information to keep from getting on the uncooperative side of the local law when he was in their town. It made working together an easier arrangement.

"Seems like a lady—a real southern lady."

"That she is, but don't underestimate her ability to sweet-talk her way into making you forget she's gotten herself on the wrong side of the law."

Layton laughed as he dug into the food basket. "How long do you plan to keep her here?"

"A day or two. I'm waiting on a train and a telegram."

The women carried on as if they were old friends visiting over tea and cake, and Nick tuned an ear to their conversation while only half-listening to Layton drone on about the snowstorm and how it compared to every other snowstorm the town had seen in the past twenty years.

Mrs. Wallace said, "Now, Miss Lainie, I'll be back around one with lunch. When I bring supper, I'll have everything you need to freshen up. It'll be quiet then, and there shouldn't be any extra people coming in and out. I'll stay to make sure you have all the privacy you need."

"Oh, that is so kind and generous of you, Maudie. It is frightfully depressing in here. And thank you so much for the extra blanket and pillow. Why I nearly froze to death last night with just this piddling piece of cloth for warmth, and the pillow— Well, it is simply unfit to lay one's head upon."

"There, there dear. What else can I get for you to help pass the time?"

"Let me think. I do have my books to keep me company, but if you wouldn't mind, perhaps you might convince Marshal Foster to let me have the deck of cards in my reticule. I'm skeptical of their use as a weapon, but no doubt he will think otherwise if I ask. My personal effects are just over there by the chair."

Mrs. Wallace made a derisive, scoffing noise of displeasure. "Of course, dear. I'll get your cards myself. We won't even ask him."

Nick shook his head at the exchange, poured a cup of coffee from the pot setting on the flat plate of the wood burning stove, and then moved to the window to wait for Mrs. Wallace to leave. When she was gone, Nick pulled up a chair facing Lainie's cell, and sat down. Seated at her small table, she continued picking at her food without acknowledging he was there.

Not knowing what else to say, he got right down to business. "I sent a wire to the Charlotte police and to my headquarters that you're in custody. I'll get a reply with instructions on how to proceed from here. It may be a couple of days before we leave."

Wordless tension hung thick between them. Murder suspect or not, Nick didn't like Lainie on the wrong side of the bars, nor did he want to leave, but sitting in silence wasn't a pleasant way to spend time with her. The worst she could do was to ask him to leave, so he threw out the questions that had kept him awake last night.

"Tell me how your husband died. What did you see in the hotel that sent you on some wild goose chase? I want to know the real reason you ran out on me in New Orleans."

"It is a long and unpleasant story."

"We've got nothing but time, and I'm a good listener."

After a few long moments, Lainie scooted her chair closer to the bars and sat facing him. She held her hands in her lap, seeming to study the way her fingers entwined and in no apparent hurry to talk. When she finally looked up, the tight set of her lips and the tense frown around her eyes told him this wasn't easy for her to talk about.

"To understand where I am today, you must know something of where I began. I come from a southern family with a long and successful business in merchant trade, and they have the money to show for it. I grew up the youngest, with three older brothers—and with every luxury and privilege. I was in my third year of university study in London, and not yet twenty, when I met Seaton in a chance encounter. Despite the considerable difference in our ages—so much that people found it scandalous—we fell in love immediately." A shadow passed over her face. "I wrote home that I was bringing my fiancé to meet them. Seaton was not met with open arms. My father refused to give his consent and disowned me when we married the next day."

"Leaving your family like that couldn't have been easy."

She gave him a little sly smile. "Oh, but it was. Seaton treated me fine...just fine. We had such good times. He liked to say I kept him young. We gambled all over Europe. Then, in time, and circumstances being what they were, after nearly nine years of marriage, we'd decided to settle in one place. Seaton wanted to live in America, and he was fond of Baltimore, so we were staying in a hotel there while investigating property to purchase.

"The night before he was killed, we'd spent a delightful evening playing poker at the hotel, and we had no reason to expect anything different the next night. On the second night, I retired early as I wasn't feeling well, so I didn't witness the shooting, but I was with him when he died."

She was quiet for many seconds. "And I will always be grateful for that small blessing."

Nick waited, watching and wishing he had something to say that would help.

"There was a cursory investigation after two witnesses swore statements that Seaton was involved in an argument over the winnings. These witnesses identified the man that shot Seaton, whom they said ran immediately from the hotel. Quite conveniently, the witnesses and Seaton's murderer all met their own ends rather mysteriously before daylight. The police were satisfied the killer had been found, albeit dead, and an investigation was not pursued."

"Why are you searching for your husband's killer if he's dead? This doesn't make sense."

"The man who pulled the trigger is dead. The man responsible for arranging Seaton's murder is a powerful man with money, important influences, and the arrogance that comes with always getting what he wants regardless of his methods for achieving his nefarious ends. And he is still alive."

Nick nodded as he worked through all the details and ramifications of what she hadn't said while working into his thinking any possible way he could help her.

"There's another piece to this intrigue."

Nick waited, giving her the silence she needed to explain in her own time.

"I believe this man is also responsible for Dean Saunderson's death."

Nick sat back, his mind jumping from one thought to another. "Why do you think that?"

Lainie held up her hand. "Please don't press me for more. Maybe sometime... But not now."

It took everything he had to back-off. "All right, but Lainie, you need an attorney. There's a law firm in Charlotte. They're expensive, but they take on tough cases. I can send a telegram on your behalf now, and they'll get to working on your defense today. You probably won't have to spend any more time in jail."

"No doubt, you're referring to Welton and Myers."

Lainie's eyes shone with a gleam Nick couldn't peg. Not quite amusement, yet it hinted of a private joke.

"Yeah." There was so much she wasn't telling that he wanted to know. "What's behind that smirk?"

She waved him off. "Nothing I'm willing to explain at this moment. I will say, however, that I am acquainted with the firm, and if I need legal representation, I will consider them."

Standing, Lainie wrapped her fingers around the cold metal bars. Nick came up with her and put his hands over hers, sorely regretting the iron barrier that separated them.

"Nick, justice will not be done unless I see to it myself."

"Justice is for the courts to handle. Get a lawyer, tell what you know, and leave the rest for the law to make right."

"The legal system abandoned me in Baltimore, and it wants to persecute me unjustly for what happened in Charlotte. I have no faith in the law, only in myself."

"That will get you a prison sentence, for sure."

"Oh, but you're wrong. I will not go to prison. One more week, not even that long, is all I need. Everything I've planned, all that I've sacrificed, will come to an end in a few days. How can that be too much to ask?"

It took all of his fortitude to keep looking her in the eye. "I can't, Lainie. I just can't."

"Then there is nothing more for us to discuss." Slowly, she backed away.

He had a sinking feeling what hope there had been for their future died with those words. Swearing under his breath, Nick pulled down his hat brim and turned up his collar, then left the building with no particular destination in mind.

***

Lainie looked up when the outer door opened, hoping it was Nick despite the terse words she'd last spoken, but what she heard was Rutherford Tolliver's smooth-as-silk voice asking Layton if he could have a few minutes alone with her.

"I'll see if she's up for visitors. Wait here." Layton appeared in the doorway, averting his eyes. "Miss Lainie? Are you decent? There's a man here who says he knows you. He wants to talk to you."

Ford would gloat that she was behind bars, but she wasn't going to give him the satisfaction of being turned away. Fortifying herself to face Ford, she said, "Thank you, Layton. Please show him in." Prisoner or not, she would receive Rutherford Tolliver as befitted a lady of her upbringing.

Layton motioned, and Ford's footsteps clicked on the rock floor in his approach.

"Gotta check you for weapons."

Tolliver held out his arms. "Certainly."

Layton patted Tolliver's pockets, found nothing, and stepped aside for him to pass. "Mind your manners. I'll be listening."

Lainie continued the Patience game spread on her table, purposely ignoring Ford, although able to observe him peripherally. The familiar hollow emptiness, the cold loathing she harbored toward him, knotted in her stomach.

Ford watched her for a minute or more before he spoke. "I remember the first time I saw you. It was Madrid. I followed you to Venice, so I could meet you in person. You were the most stunningly beautiful and fascinating woman I'd ever seen. You still are. Age cannot wither her, nor custom stale her infinite variety. Other women cloy the appetites they feed, but she makes hungry where most she satisfies." Ford fell quiet again. "You're even more beautiful behind bars, if that's possible. There's something sensual and appealing about a captive woman. She's trapped. Vulnerable. Totally at a man's mercy." He studied the unlit cigar he held between his fingers. "Helpless."

Lainie sensed more than saw his dark, predatory gaze upon her. Continuing with her card game, she let the seconds tick off. Satisfied she was in control, and her voice was steady, she raised her head, and met his lusting scrutiny and smirking confidence straight on with her own self-assured smile.

"I am no more helpless than Cleopatra. Making assumptions without a basis upon which to draw will lead to your ruin."

He clipped one end of the cigar, clamped the uncut end between his lips, then struck a match, and held the flame to the end as he puffed. When the end glowed to his liking, he said, "Too bad you're going to miss the game."

Years of gambling had taught her to conceal her emotions, mask her thoughts, and present an impassive exterior. Even so, it took all of her fortitude to access those skills right then. The hate she harbored for Rutherford Tolliver swirled inside her like thick gray tendrils of phantom smoke, wrapping around her heart and choking her with remembered pain and loss.

She'd sacrificed so much since Seaton's death; she feared she couldn't maintain the physical and emotional vigilance needed to keep her vendetta alive much longer. She wanted her life back. She was so close now, but one misstep, her world, her hopes and dreams, would crash around her. Determination pushed her courage past the sick churning in her stomach. This was a game she would not lose—not the one she now played with Tolliver nor the one in Denver. Gathering the cards into a neat stack, Lainie left her little table and faced the demon that lived in her nightmares.

"Even if I do miss the tournament, there will be other games." She lied. This was a once-in-a-lifetime opportunity, the game of the century, and they both knew it.

He drew on the cigar, exhaling sweet blue smoke that hung in the still air. "Not like this one. Thirty hours of straight poker. Thirty players by special invitation. Thirty-thousand-dollar entry fee. And one winner."

He took a step closer, his gaze boring into her with the intent to intimidate in his gloating that she was behind bars, and he wasn't. She wanted to look away, but she forced herself to meet him stare for stare, grateful that the sinister gleam in his eyes wasn't the last thing Seaton had seen before he died

"The rumor around town is a marshal arrested you on suspicion of murder."

"Well, word does get out quickly in these small towns."

"Yes, it does. But I know a little more about this than you realize"

"What do you want, Ford? Surely, you're here for more than the puerile pleasure of seeing me in jail."

He lowered his voice. "I know what happened in Charlotte. I can guarantee a verdict of not guilty to the Saunderson murder. I can get you out of this mess, Lainie. I was in that poker game, remember? All you need to do is throw-in with me."

"How can I forget, and is that a proposal of marriage or of perpetual servitude?"

He grunted a laugh. "Partnership, Lainie, partnership. Together we can rule gambling in Europe and America."

"I've already done that—with my husband."

Unfazed, Ford said, "And there would be personal benefits to sweeten our professional arrangement."

"Oh? To what personal benefits do you refer?" She knew well what he meant. She simply wanted him to say it aloud.

"I'm not a marrying man, but for you, I might be persuaded to change my bachelor status. At any rate, you'll never want for a thing. You'll have the finest luxuries my money can buy."

On a flippant head toss, Lainie retorted, "Until you tire of me. You're cut from the cloth of men who like their women young and grateful, so you trade often."

He laughed outright. "You're wrong. I like independent women who can think for themselves and who demand the respect that goes with it."

From someone else and under different circumstances, the words would have been sincere. "You cannot guarantee I will be found innocent of a murder—that you know as well as I—that I did not commit."

He waved his hand as if brushing away an annoying insect. "An insignificant detail. I can take care of the Charlotte problem under the conditions I've already offered or with a reasonable variation."

Lainie casually returned to her table. With her back to him to hide her trembling hands, she took several sips from her water cup to buy the time she needed to think. "What influence do you have in Charlotte that can assure my innocence?"

"I can produce a witness who will testify he saw Saunderson at your hotel room door, heard his blackmail threats, and that you called his bluff with your own threat to expose certain sensational details about his personal life.

"This witness will further swear the discussion continued in Saunderson's room in your efforts to help the poor young man sober-up rather than have him arrested for disturbing the peace. Then later, when he was alone, and in a state of extreme despair, he carelessly laced his whiskey with too much laudanum."

His fabrication intrigued her. Turning, she looked at him for a few moments before returning to the cell bars. "That is quite a story, but the only one in the game second-dealing was you. Other than Dean did come to my room, and it is no secret that I then accompanied him to his—where I left him very much alive—the rest is too farfetched for anyone, including a jury, to believe."

Ford knocked ash from the end of his cigar. "That depends upon the witness."

A crawling sensation tingled her scalp and scuttled down her spine in a shiver of foreboding. "So what exactly will you testify to?"

Ford grinned. "Now that's what I like about you, Lainie. You're quick. Smart. You don't bother with unnecessary details. Some men don't find intelligence attractive in a woman, but it's what I admire most about you."

"Save your compliments for someone who appreciates them. Answer my question." Lainie rested her hands lightly on a horizontal bar.

"Let's just leave it that the judge will slap your hands for withholding evidence; the newspapers will have a heyday at your expense; but you won't go to prison. That, I can promise."

Calm settled upon her. "You are correct. I will not go to prison for Dean Saunderson's murder, but not because you have intervened on my behalf. I will never be beholden to you. The only thing I want from you is retribution. And you know perfectly well of what I speak." There. She'd said it. She'd all but accused him of killing Seaton.

Ford's eyes gleamed with mocking amusement. The clock out front chimed the hour, and Ford turned an ear toward the sound, the expression on his face entirely too cocksure. Reaching inside his coat, he said, "Somehow, I doubt that's all you want from me." When he brought out his hand, a golden pocket watch attached to a heavy golden chain lay cupped in his palm.

"Beautiful, isn't it?" Flipping open the ornately jeweled and filigreed cover, he made an embellished production of checking the time. "I imagine the sentimental value alone is...priceless."

Her legs would have folded had she not grasped the iron bar to hold herself upright. As it was, she followed his every movement, hating herself for the pleasure that gave him. She'd sat at many poker tables with Ford since that day in New Orleans, and not once had he shown the watch. From that chance moment in New Orleans when he'd paused in the hotel lobby to check the time, unaware she was even in the same town, much less watching from a few feet away, she'd followed his same gambling circuit. That his name was on the roster of gamblers invited to the tournament was the reason she was playing in Denver at the end of the week. She'd embarked upon a journey down Vengeance Road, and reclaiming that watch was the prize at the end. And he knew it.

Duplicitous bastard.

Pocketing the watch, Ford tipped his hat. "Too bad you won't make Denver. We could have painted the town red." At the doorway, he paused and looked back. "My offer stands indefinitely." He took another pull on his cigar, exhaled, and watched the smoke rise. "Maybe I'll see you in Cincinnati or New York after that, or even Barcelona by fall. At any rate, I'll be expecting you." As he walked away, he added a parting twist to his verbal knife. "No doubt you'll want to talk more about my watch."

Lainie pressed her face to the bars, her fists clamped around the thick, unyielding iron. She grieved the loss of that watch almost as much as she mourned the death of her husband.

"Rutherford Tolliver. I swear on Seaton's grave and on the life of the son he didn't live to see, I will ruin you if it's the last thing in this life I ever do."

Chapter Five

Nick spent another guilt-ridden night for leaving Lainie locked up two nights running. He'd gotten out of bed countless times to go to her, and each time he'd thought better of it. Waking her in the middle of the night just to ease his conscience wouldn't fix anything between them.

Just before daylight, Nick headed to the lobby, and a sleepy-eyed clerk greeted him.

"Good morning, Marshal. I was coming up with a telegram for you."

"Thanks." Nick opened the sealed envelope and saw right away it was from his headquarters.

Developments in Saunderson case. Victim left heretofore unknown evidence possibly identifying murderer. Authenticity verification underway. Suspect's statement imperative. Relay to suspect Welton & Myers law firm has taken defense. Maintain constant protection. Sparks arriving from Julesburg to assist with escort. Bring suspect to Charlotte immediately. Report daily. Will advise accordingly.

Hitting the street at a brisk walk, Nick headed for the jail. With Julesburg not a hundred miles away, he expected A. J. with the next westbound, but there was no telling with the haphazard train schedule.

When Nick opened the door, the ominous, empty chill of an hours-dead fire in a cold building prickled his skin. "Hollis? Lainie?"

No response. Shucking his revolver, Nick swept a keen eye around the room. Everything was as he remembered from his last visit. No sign of struggle. Nothing out of place. All rifles and shotguns in the gun rack. No— The ring of keys was missing from the nail. His mouth went dry; icy dread crawled across the back of his neck. Maintain constant protection. What would he find on the other side of the rock wall? Damn it! His hardheaded pride had brought her here, and he cussed himself for leaving her alone.

Moving on cat feet, he hugged the rock wall as he inched his way to the opening into the cell area. A whisper of movement stopped him. He held his breath. Something moved again.

Nick leaped through the doorway, threw himself to the side in a crouch, eyes searching for a target, .44 clamped in his fist. But what he saw didn't agree with what he'd expected. He walked to Lainie's locked cell and peered at Hollis where he sat on the edge of the narrow cot, head in his hands, elbows on his thighs, staring at the floor. Relief washed over Nick that there were no dead bodies, but Lainie's absence still scared the hell out of him.

"Are you hurt? Where's Lainie? What happened?"

Hollis lifted his arms in a helpless, wordless gesture of explanation. His mouth opened and closed on a halting attempt to speak. "Gone. Right out— Right out the front door. Last night."

Bounty hunter? Nick's stomach knotted. "Did someone take her?"

Hollis shook his head.

Nick was as relieved as he was perturbed that Hollis wasn't giving enough information. "Where's the key so I can let you out?"

Hollis pointed. "On that chair with my pistol and the note she left for you."

Nick unlocked the cell door, and Hollis made a bee-line for the wood stove. Nick read Lainie's note as he followed Hollis

Nick,

Do not blame Hollis for succumbing to the shameless flirtations of a woman determined to be free. I know you are duty-bound to arrest me again, so I will make it as trouble-free as possible, not that I doubt your tracking skills. After all, you did find me in this quaint little cow town. The poker tournament begins on Friday at noon at the Cartland Hotel in Denver. I have a suite reserved, so you will have a place to stay when you arrive. Four days more—it's all I need. If you love me—and I know you do—you will grant me that.

Lainie

P.S. Now, aren't you glad it was not your reputation I sullied with my little getaway? I'll want my derringer back when I see you next. It would be a tragedy to break up the set.

He muttered to himself, "Damn it, Lainie. Why do I let you do this to me?" Pocketing the note, Nick leaned on the edge of the sheriff's desk, arms folded across his chest. "All right, Hollis. Tell me what happened. Don't leave anything out." His thoughts were already miles down the road planning what he had to do.

Hollis talked as he built up a fire. "Well, after you stopped by last evening, Maudie brought in Miss Lainie's supper then came back for the dishes and stayed to visit with her. After Maudie left, I checked-in on Miss Lainie from time to time, but she was just sitting there at her table with her deck of cards."

"She didn't say anything? Didn't talk to you?"

"Oh, well, yeah. She was always as polite and ladylike as could be. She thanked me for worrying about her comfort, that sort of thing. She asked when I thought the next train east would come through, and I told her that westbound trains were running at night until those tracks at Laramie are fixed, which swapped the east and west schedules."

Nick perked up. He saw right away what Lainie had gone fishing for.

Hollis rubbed his hands together over the top of the stove. "What did she promise if you'd let her out?"

"She didn't promise anything." Hollis made a sheepish glance toward Nick. "She...she... Oh, hell, Marshal, she asked if I could help her with a button on her shoe." Hollis babbled on. "It was one of them black leather expensive over-the-ankle Paris boots with high heels I've seen in a mail-order catalog."

Nick blew out a sigh of I've-been-in-your-situation. "It didn't occur to you at that time of night she would be taking off her shoes to prepare for bed rather than putting them on?"

Hollis's mouth hung open. "So help me, Marshal, that didn't even cross my mind."

Nick chuckled. "Don't be too hard on yourself. I imagine you opened her cell door, left the key in the lock, and went in to help her."

Hollis nodded. "She had her foot up on the chair and her skirts pulled way back high over her knee, and she was wearing black stockings and a garter..." He couldn't look Nick in the eye.

"Showed some leg, did she?"

Hollis sawed a hand across the back of his neck, shuffling from one foot to the other. "It weren't my fault, Marshal. She said a lawman oughtn't to be afraid to help an unarmed, defenseless woman."

"Lordy, kid, she's a gambler. Hell, she lies for a living."

Hollis cringed, and Nick shook his head, sympathizing with the hapless young deputy.

"But despite the distractions, you did manage to get her shoe taken care of, and then she kissed you on the cheek, called you a sweet dear, and lifted your gun."

Hollis's jaw dropped. "That's exactly what happened. You must know her pretty well." He was visibly relieved another man understood his humiliation.

"Yeah, I know her." The raw wound along his hipbone was a constant reminder of just how well he knew her. "What time did she leave?"

"About ten-fifteen. I remember looking at the clock, because I'd just heard the westbound whistle when she called me to...um...to..." His eyes went wide with the dawning realization.

"Interesting coincidence that she was fully dressed and had shoe problems right about the time a train arrived."

"Oh, hell, Marshal. I'm sorry. If the sheriff wasn't gone, there'd have been two of us workin' at night since we had a prisoner and...." His words faded on a shrug.

"Why didn't you holler for help or make some commotion? Someone was sure to hear you. We might have been able to catch her before the train left."

Hollis mumbled, "I was too embarrassed. I knew you or Layton would be the first ones here this morning. I didn't want the whole town knowing any sooner'n they had to."

"Well, Hollis, the whole town's going to know anyway. Take their ribbing as best you can." He didn't blame Hollis for letting Lainie get the better of him; he knew her shenanigans first hand. "I'll take care of this."

"You know, Marshal, I had a lot of time to think last night, and it came to me that her leaving the way she did might have something to do with the visitor she had yesterday afternoon."

Nick stopped at the door and turned slowly. "Who was it?"

"Well, I wasn't here, but when I came on duty last evening, Layton said that gambler feller who's been around town—Rutherford Tolliver—had come in to see her. Then after he left, Layton thought he heard Miss Lainie crying. He checked on her, but she said she was all right. Layton mentioned it to me just so I'd keep an eye on her. I think maybe that's why Maudie stayed with her so long after supper, too."

"Thanks, Hollis."

Nick started toward the telegraph office to send a message to headquarters about Lainie's escape, but changed his mind before he got there. He knew where to find her, so he reasoned she wasn't really on the loose again, and until a train came through, all he could do was wait anyway.

Walking on to the restaurant for breakfast, Nick mulled over Tolliver's visit to Lainie, and why she'd been upset after he'd gone. Lainie wasn't a crier. Whether it was her gambler's training or just a natural part of what made Lainie Lainie, he did know she wasn't the outwardly emotional type. Whatever the hell she was up to, he hoped it didn't get her in worse trouble before he caught up with her again.

***

Nick arranged to leave his horse at the livery and feed stable until he passed back through town. He'd lost count of all the times he'd done that or ridden in a stock car with his horse as he'd chased Lainie all over hell and creation. From there, he stopped in at the telegraph office with instructions to have any messages sent on to the Cartland Hotel. The rest of the day was spent at the sheriff's office waiting for the next westbound. If A. J. wasn't on it, he'd go on without him.

When the train came in, Nick wasn't disappointed when his oldest friend and mentor stepped off. They shook hands and A. J. slapped Nick on the back.

"How ya been, kid?"

"Good, you old coot. I heard you'd tangled with some rustlers down around Platte River City."

A. J. squinted at Nick, the laugh lines around his eyes deepening. "Well, five of 'em put up a pretty fair fight. Three lived to tell about it in court."

Nick grinned. "I'm sorry I wasn't there."

A. J. grunted. "Hell, you'd have just been in the way." His thick and bushy, mostly gray mustache twitched around a friendly grin.

"This is a water stop. We've got time for coffee. The restaurant's been staying open late while the trains are off schedule. It's right down the street."

"Whatever you've got going on had better be damn good. I was pirootin' with a pair of buxom redheaded sisters when I got the telegram to come help your sorry ass."

Nick laughed at A. J.'s put-on gruffness. They'd been friends for more years than they'd been deputy marshals together, and they knew each other well. "I'll be sure to send them an apology."

"You do that. And make sure you include some chocolates." He slapped Nick on the shoulder. "Now, tell me about this prisoner you've got locked up. All I know is we're supposed to escort a murder suspect back east."

Nick opened the restaurant door for A. J. to go in first. "It's Lainie. I caught up with her here."

A. J. stopped in the doorway, absorbing that information as he looked Nick over with narrow-eyed admiration. "Well, I'll be go to hell. You finally caught her, did you? I figured when it came right down to it, you'd help her leave the country before you could bring yourself to arrest her."

Nick followed him to a table. "If I'd have found her in San Francisco, I'm ashamed to say I might have put her on a boat and done just that." To the waitress, he said, "Just coffee, please."

A. J. removed his hat and put it on the empty chair beside him, then ran fingers through his mass of silvery shoulder-length hair. "I like that sassy little filly. How'd it go when you arrested her?"

Nick shrugged offhandedly, hesitated just a tad too long, and A. J. read his own meaning into the silence.

"Is that your conscience eating at you for throwing her in jail?

"That, and she— Well, yeah. It was tough seeing her on the other side of the bars."

"I'll be damned. She shot you again, didn't she?"

Nick flashed him an irritated glare.

A. J.'s roaring laughter turned every head. "You are head over ears in love with that gal, that's for plumb sure."

Nick gave in to a grin. "Yeah, I've got it so bad, I proposed to her from the opposite side of the bars."

A. J.'s eyebrows shot up. "How'd that go?"

"Depends on how you interpret there is nothing more for us to discuss." Nick showed A. J. the telegram.

Whistling, A. J. said, "She must know something mighty important for Welton & Myers to take her on as a client."

"It gets even more interesting. Read this." Nick traded the telegram for her note. "She hoodwinked the deputy and broke out last night. She doesn't know about the telegram."

"I've heard about that poker game. High stakes benefit fund-raiser for a new hospital." A. J. returned the note. "Did you report she's on the loose again?"

Nick shook his head.

"Did you wire the sheriff in Denver to arrest her and hold her until we get there?'

Nick just looked at him.

A. J. chuckled. "That's why I like working with you. It's always interesting. What's your plan when we catch up with her?"

Nick smiled, but not from amusement. "I'll decide that when we see her. She still has a derringer. It's double-barreled and, so far, she hasn't missed what she's shot at."

Chapter Six

Lainie knew well the influence of impressions that accompanied first meetings, which is why she wasn't walking into the Cartland Hotel looking the least bit travel weary. Taking her time to freshen in the ladies room in Denver's Union Station, Lainie changed into the clothing she'd carefully packed just for this occasion. With particular attention, she put every hair into place and touched-up the hints of color on her lips, eyes, and cheeks then finished off her toiletry with a dab of perfume behind each ear. With one last assessment in the full-length mirror, Lainie repacked her two leather bags, and made her way across the station lobby to hire a Hansom cab for the drive to the hotel.

During the short trip, Lainie's mind wandered again to her recent escapade in Pine Tree Buttes. Her amusement increased with each remembering, which didn't make her any sorrier for tricking Hollis. The only damage done was to his pride, and that would heal with the telling and retelling of her breakout, which would gain embellishment each time. Her conscience gave her a little twinge of guilt, though, that she'd left Nick again without telling him the truth.

He was so like Seaton, yet so totally different, if that were possible. They didn't resemble each other save their tall, broad-shouldered, trim physiques. Nick was darker-skinned, rough-hewn and rough-edged, whereas Seaton was fair-haired and aristocratic by birth and breeding. But at the unshakeable core of their beliefs was integrity and devotion to their professions and toward the ones they loved.

She often pondered what would have happened if Nick and Seaton had met. She liked to think they would have gotten on well. She felt blessed to be able to love them both without having to choose one over the other. Her eyes misted with thoughts of Seaton—his classical education, his impeccable manners, his kind heart. But there was also the steely nerve of the professional gambler. He'd met opponents on dueling fields more than a few times over cards. Pistols, swords—it mattered not to him.

In European gambling circles, he'd been known as the Gentleman Gambler from Grantham, and she, his Lady of the Cards. The respect and deference they'd received had been born of sincere admiration, and she had garnered the same respect and regard in her own right. For many, many good years, they'd danced, dined, and gambled across Europe.

But that was gone now, as was the family and inheritance she'd shunned in order to be with Seaton. And here she was again, willing to turn her back on gambling for Nick if it weren't for calling-in the debt Ford owed her. Until she did, the shards of her broken heart were simply scattered pieces of wishes thrown to the wind.

Lainie shelved those memories when the cab rolled to a stop in front of the Cartland Hotel. Stepping onto the street, she took in the festive decorations from the two banners stretched the width of the street—Friday the 13th Poker Tournament and Denver Welcomes Hospital Poker Benefit—down to the multi-colored flags adorning the front of the hotel and waving a welcome in the breeze. A bellman carried her bags to the front desk where the clerk's expression and the admiring glances from passersby assured her she'd done herself up properly.

"Good day, ma'am. I am Barry Johnston, the day clerk."

"I'm Mrs. Seaton Conrad. You're expecting me."

"Yes, and on behalf of the Cartland Hotel, it is my pleasure to welcome you. If I could have your letter of invitation, I will proceed with your registration."

"Certainly." Lainie presented her letter.

"Thank you." He busied himself with writing a note here and jotting a word there, then he handed her invitation to the bellman with instructions to summon the concierge. Turning the register book toward her, he said, "If you would sign, please."

Mr. Johnston explained, "Your steamer trunks and portmanteau arrived from the station, and your personal effects have been properly unpacked in your room. I am confident you will find everything in satisfactory order."

"Thank you, Mr. Johnston. I'm sure I will be quite comfortable."

"Ah, bonjour, Madame Conrad. I am the head concierge, Georges Larnéll. I have greatly anticipated your arrival." A slender, meticulously coiffed and attired man with a pencil-thin mustache that seemed out-of-place against his aquiline, almost effeminate features, bowed slightly in greeting. His French accent was pleasing to the ear, which drew particular attention to his flawless English enunciation. "It is my pleasure to show you to your room personally."

"Thank you. You are most thoughtful."

Larnéll took the room key from the clerk and guided Lainie across the lobby with a light pressure of his hand upon her elbow. "Let me acquaint you with our hotel."

Lainie had already admired the diamond-dust mirrors at the main entrance, the skylights and gas-jetted chandelier above the center of the lobby, and the impressive polished wood stairway to the upper floors, but she listened with polite interest while Larnéll pointed them out.

At the entrance to the restaurant, he paused to offer her a glimpse inside.

"Our chef and waiters are highly regarded. You are welcome to dine here, or arrangements can be made for taking your meals in your room. Now, this way, please. The view of the lobby is quite impressive from the grand stairway." He chattered on, pointing out this painting and that portrait on the walls as they walked to the second-floor ballroom. "And here we are. The tournament will commence at precisely noon tomorrow. You will need to arrive in the lobby by eleven-thirty for the welcoming speech."

Hotel staff hustled about preparing the room to accommodate the gamblers and spectators who would gather in the spacious room tomorrow. An excited shiver scurried along her arms. She and Seaton had played high-stakes games in Europe, but none held the thrill of this one. It was more than the anticipation of meeting Ford across a poker table. It was the exhilaration of playing against twenty-nine exceptionally talented gamblers. Never would she underestimate their individual skills at cards, but neither would she entertain the possibility that she'd leave Denver as anything less than being the winner.

"Now, Mrs. Conrad, if you will come along, your suite is this way on the fifth floor. From your balcony, you will find the view of the mountains a breathtaking sight."

Larnéll opened her door, and followed Lainie as far as the receiving room, while the bellman deposited her two bags and then left.

"If there is anything you need, please notify the front desk clerk. He will then alert me, and I will assist you."

"To what do I owe your personal attention?"

"For the duration of the tournament, each player has a member of the hotel staff at his or her disposal, if he or she so chooses." He held out the room key. "It is my pleasure, and honor, to offer my services—and friendship—to the Lady of the Cards."

"Few people know of that moniker, especially in America, and it has been some time since I was in Europe where it is more familiar."

"If I may speak candidly?"

Intrigued, Lainie nodded. "Please."

"Long before you married Seaton Conrad, I served as his second in duels and as his assistant."

"Oh?" A comment Seaton had made rose from the depths of her memories. "Go on."

"When I was a young man, a boy really, Mr. Conrad caught me attempting to steal his wallet. He could have had me arrested, but he saw something of value in me that I didn't know was there. He took me under his tutelage and taught me the ways of a gentleman, educated me and groomed me for a better life than the one I was living on the streets of Paris." Larnéll misread the hitch in Lainie's breathing, and he hurried on to explain. "I know this seems an outrageous fabrication—"

"Not at all. I recall a comment Seaton made that is only now clear to me. He had given a goodly sum of money to a poor waif we'd encountered on the street. He said to the boy, 'There is intelligence in your eyes, son. I see a desire for something better. Use this money to achieve that. I know you'll spend it wisely.' At first, the boy refused the money. He said it was too much. Seaton insisted he keep it, the boy thanked him, and ran off.

"Seaton watched him go, and said to me, 'He will do well. I sensed his integrity before he refused my gift. There was another young man, long ago, who was on the same path to ruin. I showed him a better way.' Then he turned to me and said, 'Remember, Lainie, ours is a fortunate life. We must be generous when opportunity comes our way.'" Lainie studied Larnéll, thinking back to that conversation. "You're the young man, of whom he spoke, aren't you?"

Larnéll inclined his head in acknowledgement. "He rewarded me handsomely for my years of service, and I have reaped financial benefits from investing those monies. He was a gentleman, and a good man. When news of his death reached me, I was unable to ascertain your location to send my deepest condolences.

"Thank you, Mr. Larnéll. I do appreciate your kind remembrance of my husband."

"I did, however, make discreet inquiry into the circumstances of his death, and I found it to be suspicious."

"To be frank, I am not at all satisfied the investigation identified the person responsible."

Larnéll weighed his words. "I, too, have a personal interest in seeing a certain gambler made to atone by whatever means, legal or otherwise, for his indiscretions in a different, yet similar situation." He made a slight nod of you-know-of-whom-I-speak.

Lainie considered his enigmatic words. "Mr. Larnéll, I think there is much we have to say to each other. Won't you stay? Perhaps we could order up tea.

A thin smile was his response.

***

It took Lainie no time at all to discover the red ribbon tied in a bow around the doorknob of a third-floor hotel room. Looking both ways to be sure no one was watching, Lainie rapped lightly on the door then removed their private sign. A few seconds later, a woman opened the door, and Lainie stepped inside.

"Oh, Muriel, it is so good to see you. How did you and Vance get on with your train travels?" Lainie embraced the woman, who held onto her tightly for some seconds.

"Long and tedious as always, but eminently preferable to stagecoach travel. We managed fine."

"He's sleeping?"

"Yes." Muriel indicated the door ajar.

Lainie went to the room and peeked inside. Tiptoeing to the bed, she sat beside the napping towheaded toddler. Smoothing his hair, she kissed his cheek, readjusted his blanket, and stole out of the room as silently as she'd entered. Then, joining Muriel at the sofa near the window, Lainie accepted a cup of tea.

"I expected you earlier in the week."

Lainie sighed. "A snowstorm and Nick Foster caught up with me in the Wyoming Territory."

Muriel stopped in mid-sip and lowered her teacup to the saucer. "Marshal Foster? Indeed. Where is he now?

"Undoubtedly, not far behind me." Lainie recounted the events of her flight.

Muriel clucked her tongue. "Your mischief is catching up with you." Her amusement faded. "Lainie. We must talk. There is more to your arrest than you know which is partly why I was concerned you hadn't arrived yet."

"Well, there is more to this poker tournament than either of us could have dreamed, so let's compare stories. Tell yours first."

"Nick has been following you. His reputation and job are both compromised if he doesn't deliver you to Charlotte authorities within the next two weeks. He was granted a limited amount of time to find you, and that time is running out." Muriel took a sip of tea.

Lainie realized Muriel was stalling. "And?"

"There is a wanted poster going out—yours—with a fifteen-thousand-dollar bounty."

Lainie's eyebrows puckered. "There was no bounty on the one Nick— Oh." She should have realized he would conceal that from her. "There is much that is clearer now."

"You realize any and all manner of opportunist will want to collect."

"Those are practically Nick's exact words." What she'd dismissed so cavalierly was now a sobering reality.

Muriel went on. "When I met with your family to talk of reconciliation, your father was beside himself that you are implicated in the Saunderson murder. He wants to help you."

"Considering our last words were not kind, it is difficult for me to believe he received you so graciously once he discovered your purpose was on my behalf."

"Your parents were overcome with joy to meet their youngest grandchild. That he is named for your father certainly helped soften their hearts."

"They've really forgiven me for dishonoring the family name?" Resentment tarnished her words.

"What is that in your voice?" Muriel scolded gently. "It was your decision to approach them."

"Yes, but only with your coaxing to make amends. Old wounds are the most difficult to heal. I inherited my father's stubborn pride in that regard."

"Which is why I acted as intermediary. I have had you and Vance all to myself since before he was born. It is selfish of me not to share him. Children need to know where all of their family roots lie."

Lainie nodded, sighed. "While I'd hoped for a reunion, it seems unlikely that my family is so willing to accept my return."

"Well, believe it. Your father contacted Mr. Welton to defend you."

"Uncle Jacob? We were close. I miss him. We exchanged a few letters during the years of my travels with Seaton."

"I spoke with both your father and Mr. Welton at length regarding the details of the murder as you related them to me. Since I did not know Nick had arrested you, I personally promised your return. If you aren't in Charlotte in a few days, your father is prepared to hire the Pinkerton Detective Agency to find you before bounty hunters do."

Lainie slammed her teacup down so hard the saucer cracked. "Damn Rutherford Tolliver! He is behind all of this. Seaton's murder. Dean Saunderson's murder. Seaton's watch—" Her voice caught. Sitting back, she gazed out the window, seeing nothing, but remembering all too clearly why she was in this mess.

"Well, I won't compromise your word or Nick's reputation. Just two more days, and it will be over. I owe this to Seaton and Vance. We both do."

Muriel nodded that she understood and agreed. "If you kill him, you will go to prison, for sure. There will be no self-defense plea. Even your uncle can't help you then. Are you prepared to live the rest of your life without that precious little boy sleeping in the next room? Or without Nick?"

Lainie met Muriel's intent gaze. "No. I am not willing to do either. My intent isn't murder. There has been more than enough of that. There was a time in the not-so-distant past when I was sure I couldn't be satisfied with anything less, but not now. I am going to do something worse than kill Rutherford Tolliver. I am going to ruin him financially, publicly, and professionally. Then I will take back the watch he stole from Seaton. If opportunity reveals his culpability in the Saunderson murder, then I will add it to my list of vengeances achieved."

"Will it be enough?"

How like Seaton she was at that moment. It was bittersweet comfort that Muriel's soft voice, her accent, her bearing and appearance, her plain-spoken manner and, most of all, her logical, rational thinking were so reminiscent of her son.

"Before I answer, I will ask the same of you."

Muriel dropped her gaze for a few seconds. When she looked up, the deep sorrow in her eyes resonated with the same pain Lainie carried inside her heart.

"Nothing will ever satisfy me for the loss of my only son."

"Nor me for the death of my husband."

"But this may be all we have."

"Yes, and somehow we will make the most of it." Lainie allowed herself a sly smile. "Speaking of making the most of a situation. The concierge, Georges Larnéll, has arranged for a capable young woman on the hotel staff to stay with Vance, so you can attend the tournament as much as you'd like." Lainie put her hand over Muriel's. "You need to witness Ford's downfall as much as I need you near when I bring it about."

Muriel's eyebrows went up in surprise. "Oh, yes, I would very much like to watch, but I think just the final game will suffice. No doubt, it will be quite an event to witness."

Lainie smiled. "Yes, I do believe it will. Mr. Larnéll knows who you are, and why you are here. He also understands it is crucial no one else knows. He is quite tight-lipped in that regard."

"Mr. Larnéll seems a decent, helpful fellow."

"He is, and in ways I am just beginning to appreciate. You see, we are not alone in our desire for retribution where Rutherford Tolliver is concerned. Let me tell you a most intriguing story of why this poker tournament came to pass."

Chapter Seven

Arriving at the hotel after a professional call on the sheriff to explain why two deputy marshals were in town, Nick and A. J. waited on the fringes of the crowded lobby watching people milling about in the minutes before the start of the poker tournament.

A. J. tapped Nick's shoulder and jerked a nod. "There she is. Off to the right. Talking to another woman."

Nick thought it odd that she wore a cape that covered her neck-to-toes, which suggested she was going out-and-about instead of preparing to sit at a poker table. She looked his way, caught his eye, and smiled. The beseeching plea in her eyes implored him not to arrest her, which renewed the battle he was fighting between love and duty. He'd fought that war all the way from Pine Tree Buttes knowing when he got here love was going to win over duty.

He nodded, and her tiny smile of thanks was worth every bit of the battle. Excusing herself from her conversation, Lainie made her way to a quieter area of the lobby, and Nick met her there.

Covering his urge to take her into his arms and kiss her until he'd chased all thoughts of this damned poker game from her mind, he blurted, "You'd already planned to escape when you goaded me into putting you in jail."

"Nick, I—"

"What the hell were you thinking when you locked Hollis in your cell? Holding a gun on an officer of the law and breaking out of jail will get you locked up for a lot longer than two days."

"Has Hollis filed charges?"

"No, he's too embarrassed." Her smirk riled him. "Damn it, Lainie. This is serious."

"Yes, so you keep insisting." She tapped the badge pinned to his coat. "I see you're wearing a target, so I'm assuming I'm dealing with Marshal Foster rather than Nick."

"With you, it's hard to separate the two. Here, read this."

Lainie read the telegram then handed it back. "New evidence? Well, this explains why A. J. is with you."

"Why do authorities want you so badly that it takes two deputy marshals to protect you, and when did you hire a lawyer?"

"My, my, aren't you full of questions?" she teased. "But this is not the time for lengthy explanations. The game begins in a few minutes and, once it does, I will cease to think of anything, but playing poker." From her small, silk and embroidered Paris evening bag, she withdrew her room key and slipped it into his vest pocket. "Fifth floor. First room on your right. You and A. J. will be quite comfortable while you wait."

"Oh, no. One of us will be with you at all times."

"I understand and appreciate your dedication to your job but, Nick, don't hover about and don't interfere. Grant me that, and when this game is over, I will return to Charlotte."

Nick eyed her. "Willingly?"

"Yes. Willingly."

"Win or lose?"

The smirk on her lips was as devious as it was devilishly smug. "Oh, but I will win."

"Lainie, I want to believe you, but you have a habit of twisting a situation around to suit your fancy."

Miffed, Lainie retorted, "I admit I have behaved rather unladylike upon occasion—and think of me what you will—but I am not a liar."

A. J. walked up, greeted Lainie, but there was no time for pleasantries. A woman standing on the landing of the grand stairway called out, "Ladies and gentlemen. Ladies and gentlemen. May I have your attention, please?"

Melodious ringing of a tapping against crystal glass brought the crowd to silence.

"Welcome, one and all. I am Mrs. Edith Squires, the founder of Denver's soon-to-be-built St. Camillus Women's and Children's Hospital, and your hostess for the tournament." Gesturing to her right, she said, "This is Mr. Georges Larnéll, the head concierge here at the Cartland Hotel. This tournament as a benefit fundraising event for the hospital was Mr. Larnéll's idea, and the board of directors embraced it whole-heartedly.

"While one hundred fifty thousand dollars has been raised to date, much of it donated from Denver's mining barons, our monetary goal is five hundred thousand dollars. This amount will allow for construction of a two hundred- to three hundred-bed facility, furnished with the latest medical and surgical equipment, which will, in turn, attract highly trained doctors and skilled nurses, who will offer the finest patient care possible."

She paused and looked over the crowd, obviously enjoying her position as the mistress of ceremonies. Applause and muttering approval flittered amongst the crowd.

Mrs. Squires waited for the talking to diminish. "I will now turn this over to Mr. Larnéll who will explain the rules of the game and also explain how we will proceed from here." Deferring to Larnéll, she stepped aside.

Larnéll bowed to the generous applause. "Je vous remerci. The participants in this tournament were invited by special invitation, and each deposited thirty thousand dollars into Denver's Rocky Mountain Bank and Trust. As a security measure, armed guards are stationed at the bank's vault for the duration of the tournament. Each player donated five thousand dollars to the hospital fund for the privilege to compete. The remaining twenty-five thousand dollars has been set out for each of the five players at the six tables in the form of betting chips. There will be one winner, who will claim the total amount of seven hundred fifty thousand dollars—which, explained another way, is three-quarters of a million dollars.

Of course, the hospital foundation will be ever grateful if the winner chooses to donate a portion of his or her winnings."

Oohs and *ahhs* rolled amongst the onlookers. In the moments waiting for the crowd to settle, Larnéll glanced over the lobby and let his attention linger on Nick and A. J. before continuing with the instructions.

"In order to further ensure a safe and honest game, the Cartland Hotel has employed additional law enforcement to oversee the smooth-running safety and security of this tournament. In keeping with that, before we move to the ballroom on the second floor, I must ask each of you to entrust any weapons you have about your person with the officers at the front desk."

Nick met curious glances as players and spectators alike took notice of the uniformed lawmen, each displaying a star on his chest. It suited him just fine that he and A. J. were assumed to be part of security.

"Players discovered to be armed or involved in cheating will be escorted from the game, their winnings forfeit, and divided equally among the remaining players at that table. Spectators who are found to be armed or assisting a player to cheat will be summarily removed from the premises. Play begins precisely at noon and will continue in marathon fashion until six o'clock tomorrow evening. Brief, scheduled breaks will rotate through the tables during the thirty hours of straight five card draw poker. As part of the price of your tickets as spectators, you are welcome to attend the reception and charity ball, the culminating activities for this benefit, which will commence at seven-thirty Saturday evening right here in the grand ballroom. I do hope each and every one of you will be there.

"The rules for play are as follows. The ante for each hand is one hundred dollars. The dealer at each table will open a fresh deck of cards once an hour. These cards were specially made for this tournament, and they bear the hospital foundation's emblem to set them apart from other cards that might find their way into the room."

Nick smiled at the incidental warning about cheating.

Mrs. Squires interrupted. "May I add that the decks of cards used during each game will be available for purchase at the conclusion of the tournament? The tournament champion will receive the deck of cards used in the final game as a souvenir."

"Thank you, Mrs. Squires. Now, as each table achieves one winner that player earns the gift of time until the final round, which begins precisely at three o'clock Saturday afternoon. If there are still tables with viable games at two-thirty, one more hand will be dealt, at which time it will be winner-take-all. When the final six players are seated for the championship game, Mrs. Squires will explain the rule changes, which she promises will make for exciting entertainment. If, by six o'clock, the game is still underway, one last hand, again with winner-take-all, will be dealt to determine the tournament champion."

Larnéll glanced at the clock above the front desk. "Ladies and gentlemen, it is now quarter-of-twelve. Please attend to last-minute necessities and reconvene in the second-floor ballroom. Contestants will receive table assignments upon arrival."

Mrs. Squires waved a commemorative tournament flag. "May Lady Luck look upon each and every one of you with favor. Let the wagering begin!"

Nick offered his bent elbow and Lainie accepted as they joined the slow-moving crowd making its way to the second floor. At the ballroom door, they met Rutherford Tolliver in the company of an exquisitely dressed and bejeweled woman.

"Well, Mrs. Conrad. Your resourcefulness for extricating yourself from incarceration is commendable. I didn't expect to see you here."

"Surely, Mr. Tolliver, you never really doubted?" Lainie crooned. "It would have been such a disappointment to miss this tournament, and I go out of my way to avoid disappointment. You see, I don't like to lose, especially by simply forfeiting an entry fee, which would have been much too satisfying for you. I couldn't possibly allow that to happen."

He smiled at her remarks then turned a sober gaze on Nick. "I don't believe we've met."

Lainie made a cool introduction. "Gentlemen, if I may? Rutherford Tolliver, this is U. S. Deputy Marshal, Nick Foster. Mr. Tolliver is one of the players in this tournament."

Tolliver assessed Nick. "Yes." He drew the word out. "Wyoming Territory. Our paths never quite crossed." To Lainie, he said, "Take my professional advice, Mrs. Conrad.

Bow out now before you lose your money and embarrass yourself."

Lainie's smile wasn't friendly. "I beg to differ. It is you who are outclassed here. I can win without cheating. You, on the other hand, haven't the skill to win otherwise." The sweet inflection in her voice contradicted the cutting sarcasm of her words.

Anger darkened Tolliver's face then a benevolent smile erased all traces of animosity. "This will be moot if we're seated at the same table."

"Would you care to make a wager on that?"

The inscrutable gleam in Lainie's eyes intrigued Nick, and the slight tilt of Tolliver's head said he didn't trust her enough to take that bet.

"Somehow, I believe I would lose that bet. But mark this, Mrs. Conrad, if we meet at the final table, you will be disappointed when it's over, and you will regret not taking my advice." Tolliver clamped the cigar between his teeth, made a curt nod, and hastened his companion out of the room.

Lainie was so still in her steady stare where Tolliver had been, Nick would have sworn she wasn't breathing had he not been beside her.

She murmured under her breath, "You have yet to taste the bitter anguish of regret."

"Lainie, are you up to something?"

She brushed the back of her hand across her forehead." A gentleman never asks a lady to reveal her mysteries. Just wish me luck."

Larnéll walked up and offered a sealed envelope. "Your seating assignment."

"Thank you. Mr. Larnéll, this is Nick Foster, U. S. Deputy Marshal. His partner, A. J. Sparks will be along directly. Please afford them every courtesy on my behalf."

Larnéll nodded in greeting. "Ah, yes. No doubt to escort you home with your winnings."

"No doubt." Lainie smiled as she opened the envelope. "Nick, Mr. Larnéll is my personal assistant for the duration of the tournament."

"Pleased to meet you," Nick greeted and Larnéll responded in kind.

"This way to your table, Mrs. Conrad." Larnéll led her to a table across the room from Tolliver, but he didn't seat her right away.

Nick followed, wishing he could see Lainie's face. She was stalling, or waiting, for something or some signal. He looked around, saw nothing of interest or out-of-the-ordinary, and swung his attention back to Lainie. Seconds ticked off. Players assumed their seats. Spectators settled around the perimeter of the tables, which was cordoned off to keep the onlookers far enough away to not be able to see a gambler's hand easily. Mrs. Squires watched the clock, and at precisely noon, she declared the game underway.

That was Larnéll's cue.

Unclasping the hook at the neck of Lainie's cape, he removed the flowing garment with a flamboyant sweep. A collective gasp went up accompanied by low murmurs and pointing. Lainie garnered complete and rapt attention as she turned with slow, deliberate intent, offering every person in the room adequate opportunity to look upon her.

Nick was among the transfixed. Never had he seen a more strikingly breathtaking sight. He wasn't a man who knew anything of women's fashions, but he recognized beauty and sophistication when he saw it. Moreover, he appreciated the distraction her appearance had on everyone there, not the least of whom were the five men playing at her table.

Her sapphire blue satin gown flared, gently draping and flowing like a shimmering waterfall over her hips, enhancing her womanly gifts. The dipping bodice revealed tantalizingly distractive cleavage. The pouf of her sleeves poised at the delicate points of her alabaster shoulders, and her black lace, skin-hugging, fingerless gloves extended beyond her elbows. Jewels woven through a ribbon the same color as her gown lay upon her bosom.

Lainie's southern drawl lifted with a sweet, melodious timbre. "Good evening, gentlemen. We've not been introduced." Larnéll seated her, and she arranged her skirts then placed her Paris evening bag on the table at her right hand. "I'm Mrs. Seaton Conrad."

Nick lost track of the conversation that ensued when A. J. came up beside him.

"Puts on quite a show, doesn't she? Even if she'd wanted to, there's no place in the top of that dress to hide an extra ace." A. J. pondered for some seconds. "You might want to talk to her about the rule against weapons."

"What weapons?" Nick frowned, looked at Lainie for what he'd missed, and then back to A. J. "She isn't armed."

"The way she poured herself into that dress and didn't quite get everything tucked inside is a dangerous weapon if I ever saw one. Hell, just looking at her I forgot my name there for a minute."

Nick tried not to smile, but failed. "Yeah, well, not all the men here are licentious bastards like you."

"I wouldn't bet the farm on that. Here." A. J. slapped two telegrams against Nick's chest. "Interesting reading."

The first was from headquarters.

Saunderson case blown wide open. Newspaper scandal. Family upped bounty by ten thousand. Will hold handbill until Monday. Not a day longer. Bring suspect in now.

Nick exhaled hard.

The second telegram was the response to his inquiry of Tolliver, and it was as lengthy as it was informative. What he gleaned was Tolliver had managed to stay on the edge of the law, just outside legal grasp in a half-dozen or more American and European murders and swindles that all pointed to his penchant for targeting and fleecing rich, unsuspecting young men. He'd been questioned and released on countless occasions without a crime being pinned on him. He lived, and apparently thrived, under the scrutiny of the local law wherever he gambled. In poker circles, he was considered cutthroat. He liked high stakes with big pots. He had a long history of cheating without being caught, and he always had money to throw away on expensive hotels, fine food, aged wine, and costly companionship of the female kind.

A. J. said, "We need to get on the way to Charlotte. Every bounty hunter in the country will come looking for her. I'm not hankering for that kind of fight, but for her, I'll do it."

Nick nodded, thinking the same thing.

"Does she know about the bounty?"

"No. Just that there's an arrest warrant for her. I couldn't bring myself to tell her about the bounty. She was hopping mad as it was that I'd handcuffed her."

"Better tell her. Might keep her from running off again."

"Yeah, I probably should. But for the next thirty hours, she's not going anywhere. Now, after the tournament... Well, that's a different story, but she just promised me she'd return to Charlotte after the game of her own free will."

A. J. cocked an eyebrow. "And you believe her?"

Nick blew out a tired breath. "No, but I can always hope. We'll take the early train on Sunday morning." He slapped A. J. on the shoulder. "I'm all in. I'm going to Lainie's room for a couple of hours. Keep an eye on her."

***

Nick returned to the ballroom and sent A. J. out for the hot meal he'd been grousing about since Cheyenne. After taking a turn around the room and stopping to visit with deputies stationed here and there, Nick got a cup of coffee and sandwich from a waiter and positioned himself near enough to watch Lainie play, but not so close as to distract her.

It didn't take him long to see that poker was truly her passion; she loved playing for the sake of playing. Despite being at the table for hours, she appeared as fresh and vibrant as when she'd taken her seat. He noticed some telling habits, too. She rarely bluffed; she wagered conservatively; and she never reordered her cards once they were dealt to her, not even when she discarded and received new ones. The way the cards came to her was the way she played them. Only when she won did she lay down the cards in a conventional order, and if she lost or folded, she never showed her cards.

She constantly watched and observed without seeming to notice anything at all, but she didn't miss an opponent's slightest movement, twitch, or expression no matter how insignificant, and she bet accordingly. Most of all, Nick was impressed with her cordial and gracious manners whether winning or losing. She gave as freely of compliments as she did her smile, and she tipped the dealer every time she won a hand.

When she took a man's chips, she did it with such style that the man thanked her for the honor of playing against her. It was no wonder he'd heard her called the Lady of the Cards. Nick had played his share of penny-ante poker, but he'd never spent much time around the professionals who played for a living. They were a breed all their own, and it boggled him that so much money was at stake in this game, literally, for the luck of the deal.

As the night wore on, what had been noise and droning hubbub in an over-crowded room, softened into tones of rhythmic, pulsing gambling music that waxed and waned with its own tempo. Quieting his mind, Nick relaxed and let the sounds come to him.

Ante up, gentlemen. I'll call. Raise you five hundred. Damn. Pardon me, ma'am. Glass clinked on glass. Stay. Fold. I'll take two cards. Three for me. Four kings over three of a kind. Cards slapped on tabletops. It's up to you to open. Wooden chips clicked and rippled as hands raked in pots. They say fortune favors the fool. Muffled conversation contrasted with an angry voice. Cards shuffled with soft, swooshing whispers. One thing's for certain, whichever way your luck's running, it's bound to change. Laughter. A brandy, please.

Waiters carried a steady supply of spirits, coffee, and water to players and onlookers, who took food that could be eaten with fingers right at the table or chairs.

At midnight, a man at Tolliver's table jumped up, sending his chair crashing behind him. "Tolliver! You're a low-down cheating scoundrel."

Playing stopped; the crowd didn't move. Nick inched closer to Lainie as deputies closed in on the irate man.

Tolliver idly stacked and rearranged the pile of chips he'd drawn toward him. "One should be careful when making accusations that can't be proven." He looked at the man. "Men have died from lesser allegations."

The outraged gambler shook his fist. "You may win yourself rich cheating, Tolliver, but you'll pay for it someday. I hope I'm there to see it."

Two deputies escorted the man from the room, and play resumed. Daylight arrived with one table finished and, soon after, Lainie won honors at her table.

Her dealer said, "I'll take care of your chips and have them at the main table at three o'clock, Mrs. Conrad. It was a pleasure watching you play."

Nick pulled out Lainie's chair. "Congratulations."

"Thank you. Didn't I say I'd play in the final game?"

"I never doubted you for a minute."

Lainie slapped his arm in a playful gesture. "Aren't you a shameless liar?"

Grinning, Nick draped her cape around her shoulders. "Coffee and breakfast now?"

"Yes, and then sleep."

From the restaurant, they returned to Lainie's room. "My, but it does feel heavenly to be away from the table for a few hours." She kicked off her low-heeled satin slippers as she meandered into the room while peeling off a glove that she dropped onto the narrow occasional table in front of the sofa. Before she could remove her other glove, Nick closed his fingers around her hand.

"Your last words to me in Pine Tree Buttes weren't friendly. Do you want me to stop?"

"No." She breathed the word on a sigh.

He watched her face as he pulled the glove inside out along her arm and drew it off the tips of her fingers then brushed his lips over the inside of her wrist. Her breath caught; her lips parted on a soft sighing gasp. A hint of perfume caressed his senses, sending a warm rush of let's take this further along his spine. Drawing her closer, he touched a soft kiss on the tender skin at the bend of her neck, skimmed his lips along her collarbone, whispered against the point of her shoulder.

"Beautiful as you are in this dress, I've wanted to get you out of it for hours."

She shivered; her eyelids fluttered. A yielding sigh issued from her throat, urging him on. Turning her, he unbuttoned the back of her dress, and it glided sensuously of its own accord along her curves, pooling about her feet in waves of blue satin. Nick inhaled the heady jasmine aroma of her hair when she rested her shoulders against his chest and slid her hands between their bodies to rub the hard bulge of the growing strain in his trousers. Smoothing his hands down the front of her corset, he stroked her thighs then dipped his fingers between her legs.

Lainie twisted in his arms to face him with the same want and desire storming in her eyes that he remembered from New Orleans. She fumbled with hurried fingers at his trousers buttons, then awkwardly tugged his pants down as he clumsily attacked the hooks of her corset—but they managed to get enough clothing out of the way to suit their urgent needs. Backing her to the sofa, he eased her to the cushion, pulled her hips forward as he dropped to his knees and positioned himself between her spread thighs. His hands caressed her breasts. His mouth kissed the silky- smooth skin of her belly. His tongue and lips tasted the sensitive bend of her hips, moved along her inner thigh, flicked against the most sensitive part of her need.

Squirming, Lainie giggled a protest, “Don’t tease, Nick. Kiss me. Kiss me like this is New Orleans.”

Theirs had been a slow, easy love back then, and that’s how he kissed her now—as if they had all the time in the world. She wrapped her legs around him, trapping him to her body, bare skin upon bare skin. She rolled her palms over his shoulders, along his biceps, down his back, and up again. A yielding sigh of Now...I need you now, was all he needed to oblige her.

With his arms braced on the back of the sofa, Nick gave her what they both wanted, and she met his rocking thrusts with her own intensity that erupted with her shuddering moan of release that told him he had taken her to the brink of pleasure, and she'd plummeted over the edge. His own need heightened, and he wasn't far behind her.

Head hanging, breathing uneven, Nick looked down at Lainie's contented, drowsy smile.

"You do know how to get right to the point—and you do it so...thoroughly."

Nick grinned, pecked her lips with a kiss, then pulled back and collapsed beside her. "Well, I do my best to please with what the good Lord gave me."

Giggling, Lainie slapped her palm on his belly, which made him grunt and grab her hand. "Well, the good Lord was more than generous with your endowment." Sitting up, she said, "Much as I would love to bask in your arms, I haven't much time, and a bath and a nap are calling me." She gave him a quick kiss, gathered her clothing, and went to her bedroom. At the doorway, she said, "I'll need assistance dressing for the game. Shall I call for a maid, or will you help me?"

"I'll do what I can."

"Well, I hope you're as handy at buttoning and hooking as you are with the undoing."

Nick chuckled. "Can't say I've had much practice either way, but we'll manage."

Lacing his fingers behind his head, he leaned his head back and closed his eyes on a satisfied exhale to settle in for a couple of hours' sleep. He could get used to this again, having Lainie back in his life. He didn't know how he'd convince her, but by the time they reached Charlotte next week, she'd be wearing the ring he'd carried since New Orleans. If she was going to face murder charges, she'd do it with a husband standing right beside her.

Chapter Eight

Lainie arrived at the grand ballroom on Nick's arm with the bearing of a queen greeting her subjects. In her mind, she was a queen—queen of the poker table, the Lady of the Cards. Her form-fitting, high-collared, and tightly-sleeved blood-red dress hugged her willowy figure. Her hair, done up in a smooth, almost severe style, was a bold contrast to her earlier appearance of feminine vulnerability with soft, bouncy, girlish curls framing her face and gracing her neck.

Now, as before, she turned every head, but there was decided difference in her manner, and observers responded accordingly in their hushed voices and guarded pointing. Gone was her easy, congenial, almost helpless façade of a few hours ago. This Lainie was dressed for combat, and the color of her dress professed the method by which she intended to win.

Nick left her at the table and joined A. J. where he stood beside Muriel at her front row chair. Lainie hid her smile when Nick elbowed A. J., raised a questioning eyebrow toward Muriel, and received A. J.'s grin, shrug, and mouthed word of Later. She was doubly amused that neither Nick nor A. J. knew who Muriel really was and that, for whatever reasons, Muriel had struck up an acquaintance with A. J.

Widowed twice and still mistress of the Conrad family's ancestral Grantham manor and lands, Muriel Nickles Conrad Hamilton was Lainie's pillar of strength, her unmovable rock in the face of tragedy. She'd drawn upon Muriel's mettle and her love countless times since Seaton's death. Muriel had taken her in when she'd arrived in England five months pregnant, bereft and disheartened. And now, Muriel's presence to witness this game bolstered Lainie's nerve, heightened her confidence, and refueled her determination to ruin Ford.

But those were distracting memories she couldn't afford to dwell upon now. She shifted all her thoughts and energy into the moment. Anticipation prickled on skin with the electric feel in the air just before a lightning strike. She scanned the crowd, made fleeting eye contact with Muriel, and took a deep breath when Larnéll rested his hand on her shoulder for just a second to let her know he was there. Every inch of the room was taken up with spectators, some along the walls ignoring protocol to stand on chairs, and Mrs. Squires occupied the prime position at table-side in the midst of newspaper reporters and photographers and all of them watching from the outside of the velvet-covered rope and stanchion barricade erected around the poker table.

Lainie's perusal came to rest on Ford where he dallied not far from the table in the company of the same woman who had stayed with him throughout the tournament. Lainie wasn't attracted to him but, as a woman, she wouldn't deny his attractiveness. He was tall, well-built, and not soft around the middle as were many gamblers. He carried himself with an air of superiority that was tainted by over confidence, which showed in every part of his manner, from the intelligent depth in his eyes to the smug set of his mouth.

They'd met across the poker table many times since she'd returned to the States from her period of mourning, and in each meeting, he'd behaved as befitted a gentleman until that night in Pine Tree Buttes. She knew all the time she'd been studying him, learning his habits and tells, he'd been studying her in return. That was the mark of a professional gambler. But did she know him well enough to best him?

Ford removed the golden watch from his pocket and opened the lid. He meant to throw her off-stride, ruffle her composure, by taunting her with what he possessed and she did not. He didn't know that his ploy might have worked had it not been for the information Larnéll had shared during a break in play last night. Ford was in financial trouble; he had to win this tournament to stay out of the poorhouse. This meant he would use every trick in order to win. Whether this was rumor or fact, Lainie didn't care. She intended to push Ford at every turn to keep him on the ragged edge of carelessness.

At two-fifty, Mrs. Squires welcomed everyone. "Ladies and gentlemen. I am so pleased and excited to have you all here for the championship game. Our final six players are Mrs. Lainie Conrad, Count Henri Melgar, Sir Robert Boniface,

Mr. Rutherford Tolliver, Señor Rafael Delgado, and Mr. Clyde Montcalm. Mrs. Conrad will be seated first. Gentlemen may follow as suits them, and—"

"Excuse me."

"Yes, Mrs. Conrad?"

"I would like Mr. Tolliver to sit directly across from me. I do so admire the skill he brings to the poker table, and I should like to study his technique with a direct view."

An anonymous voice called out, "So she can watch him cheat."

Muffled laughter, low comments rumbled.

Mrs. Squires stammered, "Well... ah... I suppose... if Mr. Tolliver doesn't mind."

"Surely, a gentleman wouldn't deny a lady's polite request." Lainie dared him to refuse.

"I'm always willing to oblige a lady at the poker table...and in private."

She'd expected an inappropriate response, even prepared outwardly to accept it, but inside, she bristled at his audacity. "I was sure you wouldn't mind."

Once seated, Lainie placed her evening bag on her lap then arranged her rack of chips just so in front of her, placed a water glass to her left, and the saucer and cup that would hold her coffee later in the game to her right which, when taken together, presented a barrier of sorts around her small area of the table. When she was this serious about winning, she separated herself from the other players, both mentally and physically.

Mrs. Squires continued with her speech. "This is the high-stakes part of the tournament, and, as such, there are changes in the rules of play. The first change is the ante is one thousand dollars." She paused until the excited murmuring subsided. "The next is that only one deck of cards will be used instead of a new deck each hour. I will open the deck now."

A deputy stepped forward with a lidded box from which Mrs. Squires removed a deck of cards. "As you can see, this deck is the same as the others that were used earlier." She showed the deck around, then broke the seal, tore off the wrapper, and removed the top and bottom cards.

Holding up the two cards, she explained, "You will recall during the preliminary games, the dealers removed and discarded two cards with the opening of each new deck. These are the same two cards. A difference is, one of them will be included now." Mrs. Squires handed one to the deputy who placed it into the box along with the seal and the wrapper. She presented the remaining card to the players then showed the face to the crowd.

"For those of you unfamiliar with gambling parlance, this is known as an imperial trump, a wild card. However, its value for the championship game is as a fifth ace only, which is the third rule-change." She slipped the card into a random position within the deck and placed the cards face down in the middle of the table.

Like clouds across a stormy sky, excited whispering rolled through the onlookers. Lainie's pulse quickened. She didn't like playing with wild cards. It was too easy to forget about them, and they had a nasty way of showing up in someone else's hand at the worst possible time. Glancing at Ford, she gleaned his distaste from a momentary tight frown around his eyes. Well, in this, they were alike. Neither relished the prospect of gambling with gimmicks and unknowns, and Seaton hadn't, either.

The uneasy feeling she'd had from the moment she'd taken her seat suddenly bloomed into tangible identification. There wasn't a place for a dealer. Ford realized it, too, for there was a devious gleam in his eyes. Without a designated dealer, he was at liberty to cheat at every possible turn. The game had practically been handed to him.

In that moment, the air shifted, seemed to wrinkle, and she saw beyond Ford and into that dreadful night—the night Seaton had died in her arms. He'd managed to smile, because she'd made it to his side in time to hear his last words of love, weak though they were as his life's blood drained. Now, her head and heart waged war. Did she want to beat Ford badly enough to go against the very core of what Seaton believed in? Honesty. Integrity. Self-respect. But most of all, honor. The words Seaton lived by, and the words she wanted their son to embrace as a man, pulled at her heart. This above all else, to thine own self be true. To win against Ford now, his way, was not a victory.

"Mrs. Conrad?"

Lainie blinked, coming back into the moment with the realization the crowd's silence was because of waiting for her.

Mrs. Squires prompted again. "Mrs. Conrad. I just explained that the fourth rule-change is each player will deal. Are you ready to begin?"

Lainie apologized. "Forgive me, please. I was lost in a faraway memory. Yes. I am quite ready to play."

Larnéll moved into her line of view, and she read the apology on his face that he hadn't known, or he would have prepared accordingly.

"Count Henri, you have the most chips, so you will deal first." Mrs. Squires placed the white dealer's button in front of him.

The count picked up the deck and addressed his opponents. "Good luck to you, madame, messieurs."

Playing commenced, and the dealer button moved left around the table with each new hand. By the end of the first hour, Lainie was aware, as were the players and everyone else in the room, this was clearly a two-person contest between herself and Ford. They scrutinized the other's shuffling and dealing, examined the slightest wrist and finger movements, watched each other's expressions and breathing. They raised and called with caution. Lainie folded on both a flush and a full house then took a substantial pot with only three of a kind.

Ford ran up the bet on a pair of threes, and Boniface succumbed to his bluff with all of his winnings. Boniface stood, adjusted his suit coat, bowed, but held up his hand in brusque declination to the photographers as he strode stiff-backed from the room.

In another hour, Lainie raked in the chips with just two pair—jacks and fives—which sent Clyde Montcalm away from the table. Play halted while he posed for a photograph, then he accepted a brandy and a seat to watch the remainder of the game. When Señor Delgado's three queens lost to Count Henri's straight, he, too, was out of the game. Delgado was a gracious loser, and after his photograph, he remained nearby with a glass of champagne as condolence.

In those few minutes before play resumed, Larnéll poured coffee into Lainie's cup, and placed a folded linen napkin beside the saucer. "Perhaps you may find this of use. Keep it close at hand." With a meaningful look she didn't understand, Larnéll patted the napkin.

Ford dealt next with a dramatic show of shuffling and riffling the cards, which brought forth awed comments from the audience and was meant to intimidate and impress, but Lainie knew it for what it really was. Under the guise of fancy card-handling, Ford adroitly positioned certain cards where he wanted them within the deck. Then, when he employed both bottom and second deal, she and Count Henri would receive exceptional hands, and Ford would expect them to bet accordingly.

Playing resumed. Lainie wasn't disappointed in her assessment of Ford's machinations. From the tight smile twitching at Henri's thin mustache, he was more than pleased with his cards. She knew well what Ford had done. He'd lured Henri into wagering with reckless zeal, setting him up for a swift and decisive kill through the hand he'd dealt to her. When the show of hands came, her four kings with imperial trump—the first time it had shown in her cards since play began and only its third appearance in any hand—took the pot. Ford reared back in his chair, anger dark on his face when he threw down a full house in disgust, but Lainie saw it as simple fakery to divert suspicion from his fiddle-fingered dealing. Henri simply folded his cards, placed them facedown, and stood. On a chivalrous bow, he took Lainie's hand and kissed her knuckles.

"It was a pleasure playing against the Lady of the Cards." He set his shoulders with pride as he addressed Ford. "I cannot, however, say the same for you." Facing the crowd, the count bowed again to much applause.

Professional gamblers accepted their wins with the same philosophy as their losses, but Lainie couldn't help but feel sorry for him. Ford had put him out of the game by sleight of hand, a simple magician's trick.

That was the real danger of playing with gamblers such as Ford. He wasn't an ace-up-the-sleeve cheater. He was a second dealer, a deck stacker, a card manipulator of rare skill whether by marking the backs or stripping the sides of cards when he could introduce his own deck into a game. If other players, or even an experienced dealer, watching the game detected his adroit bottom deals, once the cards left his fingers, there was no tangible proof to pin on him. Calling him out for cheating was not only pointless, it was generally fatal to the accuser and considered justifiable self-defense on the part of the accused. Most gamblers who knew him and met him at a poker table played accordingly, and it was woe to the unsuspecting stranger in the game.

How many men and women he'd cheated or killed, she certainly couldn't say, but she'd heard the talk. Seaton had assured her these weren't mere rumors, and he'd refused to play at the same table with Ford because of them. Had Seaton known the full extent of Ford's suggestive overtures to her in Paris and again in Monte Carlo, he'd have called him out with the sole intent to kill him, which was the reason she'd down-played Ford's advances and comments—a decision she'd come to regret. And it was this regret that had kept her awake at night ever since.

Nick caught her eye, nodded encouragement, and the skewed slant of her world righted itself. It was good having him near, watching over her. She wondered if Seaton were there watching, too, coaxing her, guiding her, reassuring her. She liked to think so. She needed to believe Seaton understood why she was at this table, facing his worst enemy, and preparing to employ every bit of gambling knowledge, intuition, and skill Seaton had taught her.

Chapter Nine

It took Count Henri longer to pose for photographs than it had for the other gentlemen, and during those minutes of idleness, Ford stood at his place, stretched, and visited with his attentive lady-companion. A waiter refilled Lainie's coffee cup. Camera flashes followed by applause signaled the game was about to resume. Larnéll assisted with arranging the chips she'd won from the last pot into her rack and, in doing so, a handful of chips toppled off the edge of the table.

As he gathered them, Larnéll whispered with some urgency, "The woman with Tolliver slipped him a cold deck. I would venture that a dealer accepted money in exchange for a used one in which Tolliver rightly assumed the same deck would be used in the championship game. The woman carried it so he wouldn't be caught with it on his person should a search of pockets occur. Do you want to stop the game? I can have him ejected, and you will win by default." Larnéll took his time arranging the errant chips into the corresponding rows of value in the rack.

Lainie's heart pounded in her ears; heat rose up her neck. Damn him! Taking up the water glass, she sipped to cover the turmoil raging inside her. His daring to swap a deck he'd arranged himself in full view of this attentive throng of onlookers was incredible. His was an arrogant confidence she couldn't fathom. She'd expected fancy finger work when he dealt, but had naively underestimated his nerve to ring-in a stacked deck.

When she'd embarked upon her mission to one day meet Ford across a poker table for a one-on-one confrontation, her only intent had been to win back Seaton's watch. Then this tournament had fallen right into her plans. But now that she could leave him financially devastated and expose him for the cheater he was, she knew there was another reason that had driven everything else.

She had to know how good she really was, and Ford was her ultimate test, both personally and professionally.

"No. The game continues."

Larnéll nodded. "As the lady wishes."

Ford wasn't the only one here skilled at parlor tricks. It was time to end this. Trading water glass for coffee cup, she took a drink, and returned the cup to the saucer. "Could I trouble you to warm-up my coffee and refill my water glass?"

"Certainly." Larnéll motioned to a waiter.

Still waiting for play to resume and taking advantage of the waiter and the other hustle-bustle in the room to distract attention from her, Lainie gathered the cards in preparation for her deal with care to keep the imperial trump on the top of the pile. Then, taking a moment to dab her mouth with the linen napkin, she dropped the napkin onto the cards, which allowed her to slip the wild card from the deck and move it undercover of the napkin where she positioned it as Larnéll had first placed it, neatly folded beside her saucer.

Mrs. Squires let herself through the rope barrier and came to the table. "Mrs. Conrad, Mr. Tolliver. I will remind you that if, by six o'clock, you are still engaged in play, one more hand on a winner-take-all bet will occur to determine the tournament champion. Good luck to you both."

The minutes ticked off toward the top of the hour, and Lainie stayed even with Ford for several hands, if not a bit behind. Lainie won with a full house. Ford came back with a straight and took the chips on the next hand. Then, she purposely folded to Ford's small four of a kind, although her own hand was better.

She requested more coffee, and Ford took his time stacking his recently won chips. Then he sat back in his chair and pulled out the pocket watch. She was ready, even eager, because this eliminated her need to call him out on it.

"That is a particularly attractive watch, Mr. Tolliver. I admired it in your possession in New Orleans."

"New Orleans?" Ford cocked his head, eyeing her curiously. "I don't recall seeing you there."

"You didn't." She smiled demurely. "The watch is lovely. I would imagine it is a rare design of which only a limited few were crafted, each one slightly different from the other. Have you ever wondered what stories it might tell if it could speak? Perhaps a wife gave it to her husband on their fifth anniversary, and she'd had it inscribed with an endearment of her affection then, regrettably, the watch was stolen from her husband's body after he was murdered."

At the edge of her vision, she saw Muriel lean forward, captivated by the exchange. Nick shifted his weight, glanced at A. J. who nodded back. The crowd watched, expectant, silent and unmoving, and acutely aware they were witnessing something beyond a mere poker game.

Ford studied the watch, considering her words. "Or it could have been wagered in a poker game and the owner lost it fair and square, but was ashamed to tell his wife the truth, and then later attempted to reclaim it at gunpoint...and failed." He lifted his gaze and pinned her to the chair with the dark piercing lie in his eyes.

Lainie wanted to laugh in the face of his taunting. "Well, by whatever means it came into your possession, I am quite taken by its beauty and the sentimental memories undoubtedly attached to it. Perhaps you will wager it with the next hand."

Ford shook his head, enjoying his advantage. "No, I can't do that. You see, I went to a good deal of trouble to acquire this watch. You're correct, though, about the sentimental value. The inscription is, as you suggested, a tender expression of love."

Keeping her voice steady in the face of his provoking, she asked, "Oh? What does it say?" The niggling doubt she carried that the watch wasn't Seaton's, but rather a cruel coincidence, would disappear once she knew the inscription. She had to know. In her mind, it would seal her belief Ford was the puppeteer who had manipulated the killer's strings.

Flicking open the watch cover, Ford said, "It's a line from Shakespeare. I'm sure it would mean nothing to you."

There it was—the ultimate torment—his refusal to tell her, but he'd assumed too much. She knew now the watch was, indeed, Seaton's. Too smug for his own good, Ford winked, snapped the cover shut, and returned the watch to his vest pocket.

Lainie drew from the deep well of her wealthy, southern breeding and forced polite, albeit curt, words, while managing to keep the tremor from her voice. "Well, you are incorrect. I have a classical education, Mr. Tolliver." She waved her hand at the wrist in little circles as if pulling up an off-handed memory. "Perhaps it's a line from *A Midsummer Nights' Dream*, specifically Act I, Scene I. 'Love looks not with the eyes, but with the mind; And therefore is wing'd Cupid painted blind.'"

"That would be the perfect endearment indeed, Mrs. Conrad." His smirk turned to a wicked smile as he removed a fresh cigar from the case on the table, clipped off the end with a cutter, and clamped the uncut end between his teeth. Gathering in the cards, he took his time shuffling. He was in complete control of the room and every person in it, and he used that power as a weapon to heighten the anticipation for the imminent showdown.

"One hand, maybe two. That's all the time we have left."

Lainie acknowledged with a slight nod. "Then let us not waste precious playing time in idle repartee."

Ford put the cards down and took the cigar from his mouth. With his free hand, he reached inside his vest and came up empty-handed. "I don't seem to find my matches." He patted other pockets. "Could I trouble someone?" An overeager spectator came forward to meet Ford's request. The man struck a match and held it to the end of the cigar. With smoke circling around his head, Ford stood and shook the man's hand. It was in that diverting movement that Ford ringed-in the cold deck.

Lainie saw him do it, because she was watching for it. It was a slick, fluid move that was lost to the untrained observer. Ford resumed the deal.

The waiting was over. Every sacrifice she'd made, every tear she'd cried, every time she'd cursed Ford's name, came down to this moment. The months of endless traveling, the lonely days and nights away from her son, the guilt for leaving Nick without explanation in New Orleans—All of it would be forever in her past in a few minutes. She promised herself even if she didn't leave this table with Seaton's watch in hand, she would have it in her possession before the sun rose on another day.

Ford shuffled, pushed the cards together, and riffled them again. Lainie recognized the false shuffle. It was an illusion of mixing the cards when, in actuality, not a card changed position. Each time he divided the deck to shuffle, he merely fluttered the corners under the cover of his hands then put the halves back in the original position. The deck was stacked, and he was keeping the cards in place. When he offered the cut, instead of rapping the top with her knuckles as she invariably did, she cut the deck—a deep cut. Her change in routine told him she was on to him, and his smile said it didn't matter. He nimbly put the halves back the way he'd offered the deck without the general on-looker being the wiser. But Lainie knew, and she was confident Larnéll hadn't missed a single exchange, either.

Ford dealt. Lainie left her cards alone until all five cards lay in front of her. Picking them up, she squared-up the edges. Keeping them close to her bodice and away from curious eyes, she fanned them just enough to see the markings on each corner. Two kings, two aces, and a deuce. Possible full house. The gamble was tempting and certainly enough to keep her from folding. They placed their bets. Lainie discarded one card, as did Ford. He dealt a card to her then to himself.

The four of diamonds was no more use in her hand than the deuce she'd discarded, but she'd expected this. Two pair was not going to win this game, not the way Ford had undoubtedly stacked the deck in his favor. Placing her cards face down in a neat stack beside her cup and saucer, Lainie moved her entire rack of chips to the center of the table. A collective gasp went up from the crowd.

"Since we must make an end to this game in a few minutes anyway, I see no reason to extend the suspense." She took a sip from her coffee cup, but misjudged the saucer when she put the cup down and splashed a dollop onto the table top. Absently, she pressed a corner of the napkin onto the spot then casually rested her hand upon the napkin.

Ford puffed on his cigar then blew out a perfect smoke ring and watched it float over the table. "Why indeed?" He pushed his chips to the center with hers. "Well, Mrs. Conrad, I have certainly admired your tenacity and skill to have made it to this point. It has been a pleasure playing against you, but you are correct. We have reached the end."

He placed his cards face-up on the table and spread them out for all to see. "Five-card flush. All clubs. Ace high." He leaned back, satisfied his triumph was complete. "And you can't beat that."

In those fleeting seconds when the crowd surged forward as one giant body with all eyes, all attention, all anticipation focused on Ford and the five cards spread before him, Lainie dabbed at the coffee spill again and deftly switched the top card on her neat stack with the imperial trump concealed under her napkin. Removing her evening bag from her lap, she placed it on top of the napkin as if preparing to leave.

She picked up her cards as she stood. "It is true a pair of aces and a pair of kings do not beat your hand."

Looking Ford dead in the eyes, she placed four cards, one at a time, face up on the table. She'd waited too long to miss the sight of utter and total defeat on his face to look anywhere but at him.

A sorrowful, disappointed moan rose up. Mrs. Squires stood. Ford got to his feet, ready to accept her bestowment of tournament champion.

Lainie's voice stopped them cold. "However, a full house does, in fact, win over a five-card flush. Even with ace high." She tossed the imperial trump onto the table where it landed face-up and skimmed along the table top toward Ford.

Silence, like the heavy space between each tolling of a death knell, fell upon the room. Ford didn't move. He stared at that last card, unblinking and uncomprehending. Only slowly did it register that he'd been bested at his own dishonest game. He lifted his gaze to meet Lainie's. The satisfaction of witnessing the disbelief frozen on his face mended a little part of her broken heart.

Then a rousing cheer lifted. People leaped to their feet. Wild applause shook the window panes. Lainie had mere moments before Mrs. Squires, newspapermen, and well-wishers descended upon her. She stepped around the table to confront Ford. He spoke first.

"There wasn't an imperial ace in the deck."

She feigned surprise. "*Hmm.* It appears this will remain our little secret. After all, it just won't do to have it known that the last two players in the game did their best to out-cheat the other. How would we ever find another honest game?" Her levity faded. "I want Seaton's watch." It wasn't a request. It was a demand.

Ford looked at her for some moments. "Tonight. Alone. Room Eight-eleven. Wear something...provocative. We'll negotiate a deal."

"I will never negotiate with you."

"Never is a long, lonely time, Lainie."

The crowd moved in, and Ford blended into the anonymity of being just one more person in the room. Nick remained at the fringes of the chaos, keeping a close watch, particularly on Ford. Lainie blew him a kiss and received his tipped hat in response. Muriel made her way to Lainie on her way out and managed to find Lainie's hand for a light squeeze of victory.

"Congratulations, Mrs. Conrad." Mrs. Squires beamed. "It was such an exciting game."

"Yes, well done, Mrs. Conrad. Well done, and well played, I might add." Larnéll offered her evening bag with a smile as he made an imperceptible nod toward her place.

Cutting a glance at the table, Lainie was not surprised the napkin was gone. "Thank you, Mr. Larnéll. Without your assistance, this would not have turned out as it did."

"And, thank you. Perhaps you will honor me with a dance, and then we will toast your victory with champagne. I would enjoy discussing the finer points of the game, especially the last hand."

"I would be delighted. And reminiscing would be grand."

Chapter Ten

"You're later than I had hoped, but certainly earlier than expected." Muriel let Lainie into her suite, glanced both ways along the hallway, and then closed and locked the door.

Lainie dropped her bags and went straight to Vance's room. After a few minutes of watching him sleep, she tore herself away to rejoin Muriel. There was much left to do, and the night was closing in on a new day.

"So, was winning as satisfying as you'd imagined? Watching you accomplish it was eminently rewarding for me."

"Yes, it was. More than I had envisioned."

Lainie described the rest of the evening beginning with donating her entire winnings to the hospital benefit fund. Had she won the money honestly, she'd have given a goodly sum to the foundation, and she'd have left Denver still quite pleased with her share, but her conscience wouldn't let her reap the benefit of money she'd won through deceit.

She told Muriel of the reporters and photographers swarming around her after the game. Newspapers would carry her name and picture all over the world. She hadn't danced in years, and Nick had swept her around the ballroom as if she were the belle of the ball. It had been a glorious evening, not the least of which was conversing with Larnéll regarding the disappearance of the four of diamonds and that Ford had not attended the celebration.

"How did you separate yourself from Arthur and Lancelot?"

Lainie smiled, almost giggled, at the allusion. "Bless their hearts, the poor dears were so exhausted from watching over me, they fell fast asleep and didn't even notice when I left."

Muriel ducked her chin and arched her eyebrows. "They fell asleep? Two deputy marshals simply went to sleep while guarding a prisoner?"

"Well, they may have had a little help."

"Help?"

"You know I often have coffee after a game."

"Yes." There was a suspicious intonation to the word.

Lainie smiled a little. "It seems after sitting up with me and drinking many cups of coffee, they were overcome with sleepiness. In fact, they both fell asleep in my bed."

It took Muriel a few moments to grasp what Lainie had avoided admitting. "You drugged two officers of the law and then invited them to share your bed with you? At the same time?"

Lainie feigned insulted pride. "Certainly not. There is barely enough room for the two of them. It is a small bed, after all."

Muriel shook her head, laughing softly. "What such good fortune for you that they fell asleep where they did of their own accord. In fact, it seems a marvel of coincidental convenience." Then Muriel's amusement faded. "You play dangerously, Lainie. If they don't wake up—"

"Oh, I was careful. When I left the room, both were sleeping as peacefully as Vance is now. They'll awaken in a few hours, undoubtedly with headaches and colorful words associated with my name. But awaken, they will."

Muriel shook her head, albeit with exasperation rather than approval. "And now?"

Lainie jutted her chin, defensive and determined. "I'm going to get Seaton's watch from Rutherford Tolliver."

Muriel nodded approval. "So. It has finally come down to this."

"It has, and it is long overdue. The end of our vengeance journey is at hand. I intend to make it a finale fitting of Seaton's memory. Then we're going to board the early morning eastbound train."

"To Charlotte?"

"Yes. To Charlotte."

***

It was the dark of morning when nothing and no one stirred. Daybreak was still just a promise at the edge of the horizon when Lainie stood in the hallway outside of Ford's door. Once more, she inspected her attire to make sure all was in place and properly concealed under her boudoir garments. Upon first dressing, she donned her woolen traveling suit, because it was the logical choice in light of impending travel, but mostly to defy Ford's desire to dress to please him. Then she'd reconsidered. Lust was his Achilles' heel. It was his weakness she intended to exploit as a means to her end.

She knew well what he would see when she removed her velvet cape—a floor-length, diaphanous, black chiffon, curve-hugging peignoir that hinted she wore nothing else beneath the silky cloth. The satin waist-length pèlerine she wore over the peignoir concealed Seaton's shoulder holsters with the pearl-handled derringers. The holster harness didn't fit her, which made it an uncomfortable accoutrement, but it was a tool necessary for concluding her business. Had Seaton been wearing his derringers as he usually did when gambling, she was convinced he wouldn't have been the man who had died that night. But the hotel had expressly forbidden weapons at the table which, in the end, had not prevented the violence that had ultimately destroyed her world.

Closing her eyes, she inhaled a deep breath, held it, exhaled slowly, then opened her eyes, and rapped lightly on the door.

"Please, come in."

On another deep breath, she opened the door. Dressed in a brocaded smoking jacket, dark colored pressed trousers, and as nattily groomed as ever, Ford stood across the room in the open doorway of what she presumed to be the bedroom.

"Where is your matched pair of deadly marshals?" He chuckled at his cleverness.

Lainie stepped across the threshold and gave the door a light push behind her. With all the bearing she possessed, she walked toward him while making a casual assessment of the room, hoping to spy the watch, but not surprised that she didn't.

"They are otherwise occupied at the moment."

He motioned toward the sofa with the whiskey glass he held in his hand. "Please, sit. We'd just as well be comfortable."

"I prefer to stand."

"Certainly. Something to drink?"

She shook her head. "I'm not here to exchange pleasantries. Therefore, I will get right to heart of my visit. I know you murdered my husband."

Unmoved, he chided in a tone used to scold a child, "Lainie, Lainie, Lainie. The man who killed your husband was found dead in the alley after the shooting."

"As were the two witnesses. Being the money behind the gun is the same as pulling the trigger yourself. Worse, as far as I'm concerned."

Her accusation amused him. "You also know I was questioned and cleared of all suspicion."

"Yes. I am aware of that, but how coincidental that you had a room at the hotel so you could be close enough to oversee the shooting from the shadows as well as witness the aftermath. And weren't you the concerned and caring Samaritan to express your condolences in front of people who erroneously assumed you were sincere."

Ford let the accusations pass. "But not convenient enough to join the poker game either night you and your husband played, however."

"Only because you were not invited. The gentlemen playing knew Seaton wouldn't stay at the table if you were allowed to join."

Ford's eyes narrowed just enough to gratify Lainie that she'd not only gotten under his skin, she'd rubbed salt into an open wound.

"You killed the man you paid to kill Seaton. When that plan didn't put me into your arms, then you killed Dean Saunderson so it would appear I was responsible for his death in order to put me in position of dependence upon you to prove my innocence of murder."

"You persist in these outlandish notions with such a convoluted story. If I didn't know you better, I'd think you'd taken leave of your senses." Ford grunted a mirthless laugh.

"Enough of this nattering. I want my watch."

Ford looked at her for some moments then made a slight nod over his shoulder. "It's on the table beside my bed."

Of course, it is.

"Let me show you." He downed what was left of his whiskey as he walked into the bedroom.

To cross that threshold was to go knowingly into a viper's den, but to give up now, to abandon her mission, was not possible. She was too far into retribution to turn back. Another deep breath, then a nerve-calming exhale, and Lainie moved forward. As she crossed the bedroom floor, she noted the open balcony door, felt the faint movement of the early morning breeze, saw the gentle light from an oil lamp casting its soft shadows, and understood with no misgivings, the meaning of the drawn-back bed covers.

Beside an opened bottle of wine and two wine glasses, Seaton's watch rested on the little table in a velvet-hinged box with the lid raised. It was hardly an arm's reach away. Just a quick grasp and it would be hers. But she wouldn't do that. Couldn't. He'd not let her have it so easily, and she'd not win in a physical scuffle that would end with Ford disarming her and then his taking of her body what he wanted. Waiting, strategizing, and seizing the opportunity in order to win—these were all pieces of a game she knew how to play.

"There was a time when I wanted to know how you stole it from Seaton, but it no longer matters to me. That I am here to relieve you of it is my only interest."

"Stolen... Such a harsh word."

"So is murder." She met him stare for stare. "But both are true, nonetheless.

Ford chuckled, pleased with their witty exchange. "My offer to trade it still stands."

He was so smug, so sure he had the upper hand, that for some seconds, she couldn't speak past the outrage rising inside her.

"What do I see in your eyes? Defeat? Acceptance? Or...something else? A little parlor gun in your bag?"

She almost smiled that he was justified in his suspicion. She held out her drawstring reticule that dangled from her wrist by short strings. "By all means."

He smiled, shook his head. "That you offer it willingly means it's empty and that you're here to accept my terms. I don't need to look."

"Oh, but I insist. You'll find something of particular interest inside."

"What?"

"A keepsake to remind me of the last time we'll ever meet across a poker table."

Curiosity moved him to take the bag, stretch-open the gathered top, and look inside. His amusement of humoring her faded into a tight, stiff-necked scowl. "A trump card and the four of diamonds will not go far in negotiations." He dropped her bag on the table beside the watch.

That she'd struck another nerve pleased her. "I'm not here to negotiate for what is rightfully mine."

"Lainie, we both know better. If you thought you could take the watch from me by force, you would have done so long ago. Or you would have sent someone on your behalf to claim it."

"Do not presume to know what I would or would not do based upon the methods you would employ."

"Then maybe there's another reason."

"And what is that?"

"It's not the watch you really want."

"What do I really want?"

He cut a slow, sidelong glance at the bed then back to her.

She steeled her nerve to resist shrinking from his touch when he extended a hand toward her. But in that reach, she detected a tremor, an instant's hesitation, as he unclasped the hook of her cape and drew it off of her shoulders. What did that mean? Fear that she'd reject him? Eagerness for the conquest? Disbelief that she was willingly standing before him like this? He placed her cape on the bed and stepped back. Looking her over, he covered her body with a slow sensual gaze, savoring every inch of what he saw before him.

"I didn't expect to see you dressed this...in such a revealing..." He ended his visual journey of her body with a declaration of you know you're mine now in his eyes. "Stay. Stay with me, and everything I have will be yours. Including the watch."

She didn't relish this bandying at his bedside; it was as uncomfortable as it was dangerous. "Perhaps a glass of wine on the balcony? It promises to be a memorable sunrise."

"Certainly."

At the balcony railing, Lainie sipped from her glass as she gazed toward the eastern horizon, listened to the awakening Sunday morning city-sounds, heard nearby church bells ringing their call to early worship. Ford turned his back to the sky and rested a hip against the railing.

"It's time to admit why you're really here, and what you really want from me."

That he harbored an obsession for her fueled by lust and a desire to possess her for the sole reason that she was unattainable, she knew from long experience, but when she turned to him with a scathing retort balanced on her lips, what she saw burning in his eyes frightened her, and she wasn't one easily scared.

It was love.

For the first time through this ordeal, doubt edged its way into her cold determination to achieve revenge. Dealing with lust was impersonal. It was a thing to keep at a safe distance, but facing a man's love... That was something else entirely. It had never entered her mind. For the tiniest instant, her heart softened. Had she been wrong about him? Had grief and hatred skewed her ability to see what had been there all the time? In that moment of self-doubt, she allowed him to see into her heart, into the very core of her vulnerability, and to glimpse her weakness.

Compassion.

"We can have a good life together, Lainie. I know how to treat a woman. A lady. All you have to do is say it." Ford took her wine glass and placed it beside his on the wide, flat-topped balcony railing.

She faltered. Never had she overplayed a hand; she always maintained a cool head. But now she wanted to turn from, run from, the love that showed on his face, gentled his voice, and softened his eyes. No! She told herself. Rutherford Tolliver wasn't capable of love, only obsession. Her confusion battled with rational thinking. The foundation of hatred she'd worked so long and hard to build—tear-by-falling-tear, night-by-sleepless-night—began to crumble.

Confident she was now his for the taking, he pressed her. "Lainie, the first time I saw you, I knew you'd come to me, that you'd be mine, in time. All I needed was patience and opportunity. You're here now, so I've been rewarded with both."

That was all she needed to return to the solid ground of loathing. She wasn't his; she never would be. She had been Seaton's wife, his companion, his friend, and Ford had taken him from her. And through Ford's scheming in Charlotte, she was in danger of losing Nick's love, too. "You presume much in your confidence."

"No. No presumption. I see it all over you. Your cheeks are flushed. It's in your eyes. All you have to do is ask."

He'd played-out his hand and was calling in the bets. To win, she had to surrender. Sensing the subtle change in her demeanor, Ford touched her cheek. She allowed him to draw his fingertips along her jaw and trace a line along her neck to the hollow of her bare throat. When his other hand came up to pull loose the ribbon bows on the front of her pèlerine, she took a halting step backward, crossed her arms in modest protection under cover of her short cape, and wrapped her fingers around the grips of the derringers.

"Ford. Please, no. Don't—" Her coy, baiting retreat brought him forward to capture and conquer. He grasped her arms and brought her hard against his chest. She'd broken him at the poker table, and now he intended to destroy the barricade she'd erected around her heart with what in his mind was love.

His mouth was hot on hers. She accepted the assault, tasted his lust, felt the strength of his growing need, but she gave him nothing back of what he wanted. He snaked an arm around her waist, tightening his hold, his other hand slipping under the front of her pèlerine to open her arms for him.

Turning her face, she whispered, "Not here. Not like this—"

In the moment he loosened his hold, the metallic click of the drawn-back derringer hammers stopped him.

"Release me." Inside, her cauldron of boiling hatred for him overflowed.

Ford stepped back, his smile widening with the confidence she'd not shoot him. "You don't hate me enough to go to prison for killing me. I know a bluff when I see it."

"You are only partly correct. I won't kill you, but I have four bullets, and as I am aiming from a close-range advantage, it's likely at least one bullet will find its mark and leave you with a remembrance of our last meeting." She lowered the barrels to a point below his waist. "I have been known to bluff upon occasion. However, this is not one of those times." Lainie backed through the doorway, her heart as hard as her hands were steady. "I am taking my watch. This is now over between us."

Ford lunged. "No, it's not—"

Lainie pulled the triggers. Four popping sounds merged with the tolling of the church bells. She didn't know how many bullets found their mark, and she didn't care. What mattered was Ford staggered back, stunned. The shock that she'd shot him etched in deep lines on his face. In those seconds, Lainie slammed the balcony door shut and turned the lever lock even though she knew the locked door, sturdy as it was to block wintry Rocky Mountain weather, wouldn't keep him at bay for long, but hopefully long enough she could leave town ahead of him.

Looking at Ford through one of the top-of-the-door windowpanes, she said, "This is the least I can do after you left me in Baltimore without my husband."

Lainie re-holstered the derringers on her way to the bedside table. After all this time of wishing and dreaming, regretting and despairing, Seaton's watch was finally hers. Cradling the watch in her palm, she rolled her fingers over the filigreed and jeweled top, and then opened the cover. The inscription, just as she'd quoted it to Ford, was there in the beautifully written calligrapher's hand. Then, for a few wondrous seconds, she clutched the watch to her breast before bringing it to her lips for a gentle kiss to welcome it home. Tucking the watch into her reticule with her other keepsakes, she donned her cape, and without a glance toward the balcony, she closed the bedroom door behind her, and left Ford to deal with the misery he'd brought upon himself.

Chapter Eleven

He'd been awake for several minutes, but Nick couldn't convince his eyes to stay open, which when combined with an occasional squinty-eyed look around to get his bearings, activated a pounding in his head. Even worse, his mouth was dry as desert sand when he swallowed. Giving up the battle, he closed his eyes, steadied his breathing, and let his mind settle. After a few minutes, bits of memories came back. Last night...

He remembered drinking coffee with Lainie and A. J. after the grand ball, talking about the tournament, and his plans for returning to Charlotte. It had been a pleasant, lazy couple of hours. Then Lainie wanted to pack before she went to bed, needed help moving her steamer trunks and portmanteau, and that's when things had gone all fuzzy in his head, the room had tilted, and his legs gave out. He had a murky memory of Lainie putting her arms around him to break his fall, and they collapsed on the bed. But he had nothing else until waking up.

The bed creaked, the mattress moved, the bed linens shifted, and he smiled. At least Lainie was still here, which brought up his interest in an early morning dalliance with her. Pushing past his throbbing headache, he rolled to his side, reached out to touch her, and gently squeezed her bare shoulder to awaken her.

"Good morning, sweetheart."

When she didn't respond, he stroked the length of her hairy arm, only vaguely wondering why that seemed odd.

Legs stretched, then a heavy, muscled arm lifted and draped over Nick's hip, and a raspy, baritone voice muttered, "Mornin' beautiful."

Nick blinked open bleary eyes, and A. J.'s bushy mustache came into focus just a few inches away.

"Shit! Son of a bitch! What are you doing touching my ass like that?" Nick reeled backward, clambering in a mad exit off the side of the bed.

A. J. left the bed on his side in a similar wild leap that sent bedcovers flying. "Why the hell were you sweet-talking to me?"

In the same instant, they hit the end of an invisible tether that yanked them both back onto the bed. Pain shot up Nick's left arm and across his shoulders. A. J. sprawled on top of Nick, pinning him under his naked body.

"Hey, hey, hey. Watch where you're grabbing. Get your ass out of my face." Nick heaved A. J. away and scrambled from under him.

"Damn it, Nick, don't be wrestling around when you've got a roaring jack goin' on there. Shit! What were you planning on doing with that?"

"I thought you were Lainie."

"Not very damn likely."

Metal bit into Nick's wrist when A. J. swung his arm as he sat up. "Damn it! Stop thrashing around. We're handcuffed."

"Hell, I figured that out on my own. I also figured out we can thank your lady-friend for this. Where're the keys?"

"If I knew that, I wouldn't be bouncing around here naked as a jaybird."

A. J. got on his knees on the mattress, working every way he could to get his wrist out of the handcuff, while Nick tugged and pulled at the thick, vertical bars of the heavy walnut headboard frame where the two sets of handcuffs had been hooked together on the back side of the center bar then hooked to their arms.

"Lainie!" Nick yelled, waited, his attention pinned to the partly opened door. "Lainie! Get in here with the damned key. This isn't funny." Nothing. Twisting around, he searched for the key in the bedcovers, on the floor, swept an intense gaze around the room, inspected every inch, every nook and cranny. He went right over the dressing table across the room then jerked his gaze back to it.

"There. Beside the door." Nick pointed. Keys dangled from a red ribbon looped around the top of the coffee carafe. A bit of paper with his name written in large bold letters was propped against the carafe.

"Looks like she left you a love note, too." A. J. started laughing and plopped himself on the mattress with his back against the pillows at the headboard.

"I don't see what's so hilarious about this."

A. J.'s laughing simmered to a head-shaking chuckle. "What the hell else are we going to do? I knew something was up when you passed out, and she had me help get you situated in bed. Then she got me to talking about how you and me met. I even told her what my real name is, and I haven't told anyone in..." He had to think. "Well, in a helluva long time." He chuckled again. "Even for all her shenanigans, you've got yourself a good woman in her. Stick with her and help her through this murder investigation."

"I intend to do just that." Nick waited, expecting more, but it wasn't forthcoming fast enough. "Well, what's your real name? You can't throw-out a baited hook like that and not expect me to bite on it."

A. J. looked over at Nick with a warning scowl. "You won't laugh?"

"I'm not promising anything right now."

"Amphitryon Jedidiah." He slanted a distrustful glare at Nick to see if he was laughing.

Nick gawked at him. "Am...Amphi... What?"

"My folks went on one of the caravans to Santa Fe. They had two books with them. A King James Bible and a book of old Greek stories. I was born along the way somewhere around Taos. My ma picked a name from the Bible, and my dad from the other. Hell, I was ten before I learned to spell my own damn name. It was easier to go by A. J. I didn't have to fight over some character making fun of my name."

A. J. cleared his throat. "Well, back to last night. That Lainie is a darn easy gal to talk to, and we sat here on the edge of the bed for five maybe ten minutes. Pretty soon, I was seeing two of her. Then her voice took on a sort of hollow, empty well-echo sound. The more I tried to talk, the thicker my tongue felt. About the time I blacked out, it came to me that we damn sure shouldn't have been drinking that coffee she kept pouring or downing those couple of bourbons to toast her win."

Nick worked his jaw, but no words came out. Damn. He'd been duped as easily as Hollis. He mumbled to himself, "She promised she'd go back to Charlotte after the game."

"At least she didn't shoot us before she left." A. J. laughed some more.

Nick grunted, almost chuckled.

"Got any bright ideas how to get those keys?"

Nick nodded, grimacing at the pain accompanying the head movement. "Yeah, I do. We'll drag the bed to them."

"Just how the hell do you suggest we do that with our arms hooked together?" He gave a good hard yank on the headboard.

"You stand on your side, and I'll stand on mine. We'll grab the side rail and sort of lift and drag as far as we can, then drop it, get another grip, and..."

A. J.'s you're-full-of-shit expression stopped him.

"Well, do you have a better idea?"

A. J. scratched his chin. "No, I don't guess I do."

"Grab a bar with your handcuffed hand and reach down like this with your other hand." He demonstrated and looked at A. J. who hadn't moved. "What?"

A. J. cocked his head. "That's an indecent position you're in there. You ought to see your backside in that cheval mirror over there."

"Damn it! Just grab the bed." As an afterthought he warned, "And stop looking at my ass."

A. J. laughed as he assumed the same position.

"Count of three," Nick said. "We'll lift, pull forward, take it as far as we can, drop it, and go again. Ready?"

"Ready."

"One, two, three. Lift."

The first attempt failed when the head of the bed hit the floor with a thud, and the foot of the bed stayed solidly rooted. A. J. lost his balance and flopped face down on the mattress with a grunt and string of cuss words.

"Damn it, A. J., I said lift and step, not throw your ass down on the bed."

A. J. righted himself, still cussing. "I did lift. We're off balance. I can't get the right leverage. Grab down by the foot this time."

Nick moved as far as he could toward the end of the bed frame and took a fresh hold. "Again. One. Two. Three. Lift."

This time they made several slide-steps before the bed banged down.

A. J. looked at Nick with amused dismay. "This is a big room, and that key's clear on the other side. This ain't getting any easier, and my head's none too happy about the exertion or the noise."

"You think I feel any better? Just shut up and lift."

They picked up the bed right when they heard a door in the outer room open and hurried footsteps nearing. Nick dropped his side as he whipped around. A. J. lost his hold, and the side rail barked his shin on the way down. Hopping on one foot and rubbing his leg, he stubbed his toe and went sprawling on the mattress.

"Lainie? Get in here and take these handcuffs off. Lainie!" Nick stretched, craned his neck trying to get a glimpse into the other room through the partly opened door.

Georges Larnéll burst through the doorway. "Marshal, you must come with me—" He stopped, stared. His initial astonishment turned to wide-eyed interest. "Gentlemen. This is intriguing, to say the least, and I compliment you in your discretion to conceal your affections from the public, but I fear Mrs. Conrad is in grave danger. You must come with me at once."

"This isn't what you think." Nick grabbed a pillow to cover himself and talk at the same time without achieving success at either. "We've got a problem here— Get...get the keys. On the dressing table. Over there." Pointing, he dropped the pillow and made a futile, fumbling grasp to catch it as it bounced out of reach.

A. J. asked, "Danger? What happened? Where is she?"

Larnéll snatched the ribbon from the carafe and hurried to the bed. Nick put out his hand for the keys, but Larnéll ignored him and climbed onto the mattress.

Recoiling, Nick complained, "What the hell are you doing? Get off the damn bed."

Larnéll made quick work of unfastening the handcuffs. "Had I but known your propensities—" He made a dismissive wave. "Well, now is not the time. Please, dress yourselves. We must hurry."

"We have no propensities," Nick barked. "What's going on with Lainie?"

Larnéll gathered clothing and shoved them in Nick and A. J.'s hands with disregard to the proper owner. Nick grabbed his trousers from A. J. while skittering and hopping around the room in his attempt to dress without Larnéll's persistent determination to assist.

Larnéll expounded while chasing Nick about. "Mrs. Conrad, with her son and mother-in-law, checked out of the hotel to catch the early train, which hasn't yet departed—

"What did you say?" Nick wheeled on Larnéll, grabbed the man's arm and jerked him to a halt. A. J. stopped with one leg in his trousers and stared at them.

"Mrs. Conrad, her son, Vance, and Mrs. Muriel Hamilton left not long ago—"

A. J. interrupted, "You never mentioned she had a kid."

Bewildered, Nick replied, "She never told me."

A. J. jutted his chin at Larnéll while he finished pulling up his trousers. "This Mrs. Hamilton, was she a tall, handsome woman? Light brownish hair, wore tailored, expensive clothes? Soft-spoken British accent? Proper, like an aristocrat?"

"Yes, that is an adequate description. Such a lovely woman." Larnéll tried to assist Nick with his shirt, but received a hand slap for his efforts.

A. J. went on. "And the boy was somewhere around two, not more than three years old. Towheaded, big brown eyes, talkative and friendly?"

"Oui, and there is much of his father in him—"

Nick eyed A. J. "How do you know them?"

"I had supper with them in the restaurant Friday evening. The tables were full, and Mrs. Hamilton had a waiter invite me to join her. The boy was with her. I was sort of taken with them. There was something familiar about her, but I couldn't pin it down. Now, I know. I saw her in New Orleans a couple of times, passing through the lobby, carrying a small child, but I didn't pay any more attention than that. There were other women and kids there."

Nick punched A. J.'s arm. "Why in the hell didn't you mention this earlier?"

A. J. gave him a shove. "It was on my mind, but we've been busy, and Lainie sort of put a crimp in my plans last night."

"Messieurs s'il vous plaît, écoutez-moi!"

The marshals turned as one to stare at Larnéll.

"There is no time to delay. I was an associate, and a friend, of Seaton Conrad's. Hospital benefit aside, I organized this poker tournament for the purpose of bringing Mrs. Conrad and Rutherford Tolliver together in a high-stakes poker game to give her the opportunity to— Well, it doesn't matter now. I must admit that my motives were originally strictly for my own satisfaction, but I reasoned it was the least I could do to repay something of what her husband had done for me."

Larnéll scurried about gathering gun belts and hats, which he tossed to Nick and A. J. who swapped for the right ones.

"I have always believed Tolliver was somehow involved in her husband's death, but until she and I spoke after she arrived at the hotel, I did not know she had been following him all this time in an effort to... What is the saying? To get even."

"So, you're after revenge, too?" A. J. pulled on his second boot.

"I am indeed, sir."

Larnéll grabbed hold of their arms and hustled them into the front room. On the way out, Nick grabbed Lainie's note from the dresser.

Larnéll waved the ribbon and keys with histrionic urgency. "Will you please hurry?"

"I'll take those." Nick relieved Larnéll of the keys. Nick threw on his duster, shoved the keys and note into a pocket, and followed A. J. out the door. The three men took off running for the stairway at the end of the hall.

"Tell us what's going on," Nick said.

"I was unaware that Mrs. Conrad was suspected of Dean Saunderson's murder, and she did not share that information with me, so when I read the telegrams that arrived for you, I alerted her of their contents out of fear you would arrest her. For her to be unable to play in the tournament would have been devastating to my ulterior purpose."

Larnéll paid no attention to the scowl Nick gave him as they bounded down the wide stairway three abreast.

He went on, "A short while ago, Tolliver accosted the desk clerk, demanding to know if Mrs. Conrad had left the hotel. The clerk said Tolliver appeared ill, in pain and limping. When he threatened the clerk with physical harm, the clerk admitted Mrs. Conrad had indeed left for Union Station. Naturally, when I found out, I was distressed over Tolliver's untoward conduct, but I wasn't alarmed until one of the staff then reported seeing Mrs. Conrad on the eighth-floor hallway just after daylight. While he didn't see her leaving Tolliver's room, he had heard a muffled sound something on the nature of a distant firecracker or small explosion, perhaps a gunshot, he wasn't sure, not long before he saw Mrs. Conrad."

Nick grabbed Larnéll by his lapels and shoved him against the banister. "Why would she go to Tolliver's room?" The drugged coffee and the handcuffs made sense now. Damn it to hell and her secrets. This time she just might get herself killed.

Larnéll put his hands up in defense, stammering, "I—I believe she...she may have gone there to retrieve the pocket watch—"

"The watch they had words over in the game?"

He nodded vigorously.

Nick lifted the smaller man to his toes. "What else do you know?"

Larnéll hesitated, his eyes shining with fear for his own life, but words didn't come.

"What else?" Nick shook him so hard Larnéll's head smacked the wall.

"I—I have evidence that will clear Mrs. Conrad of Dean Saunderson's murder and identify Rutherford Tolliver as the killer."

Nick swung Larnéll around and slammed him into the opposite wall, one hand holding him up and the other hand clamped around Larnéll's throat, squeezing. "You were going to let her take the blame—"

A. J. pulled Nick off of Larnéll. "Simmer down, Nick. Don't go killing a witness."

Larnéll side-stepped around Nick, but he wasn't quick enough to avoid Nick's tight grasp on his arm. "What evidence?"

"I am not a brave man. Until a day ago, I did not know Mrs. Conrad was implicated in Dean's death. You must understand... My situation is...delicate. The Saundersons are an old family, founders of the town. The scandal would ruin their good name, tarnish Dean's memory. He and I were discreet, but we'd argued over how to tell his family he was leaving Charlotte and moving with me to Denver. I had secured a position here at the hotel for him…" Larnéll couldn't continue. He looked imploringly between Nick and A. J., his face a picture of fear combined with the relief of confessing a guilty secret. "Dean and I were lovers."

Nick stepped back, his lawman's experience giving him nothing to draw upon for this.

Larnéll continued. "I have taken a leave of absence while I return to Charlotte to give testimony on Mrs. Conrad's behalf, but she left the hotel before I had the opportunity to fully explain. Then Tolliver appeared in all his fury. I went to his room, but he was gone. It appeared he'd left in quite a hurry, undoubtedly via a little-used hotel door. His larger pieces of luggage are still in the room. That is when I came to Mrs. Conrad's room to find you."

A. J. asked, "What evidence do you have?"

"It is quite complicated. Tolliver took advantage of a chance situation and used it as leverage. Unbeknownst to him or Mrs. Conrad, I witnessed both of them entering and leaving Dean's room, at separate times. There is more, but unnecessary to explain at this moment." Larnéll took a deep breath and plunged onward. "Because of Tolliver's reputation and powerful influences, I feared for my life from him if I came forward. Dean was dead, and testifying, facing Tolliver in court, would not bring him back to me."

"Why did Tolliver kill the kid?" A. J. asked.

"At the time, I could make no sense of it, but I came to understand it was to acquire, through blackmail, what he desired most. Dean was merely his unfortunate device to achieve his purpose."

Nick summed it up in one word. "Lainie."

A. J. gave Nick a shove. "Let's get moving."

They hit the lobby running shoulder-to-shoulder. People stepped aside to let them pass. They burst through the front door, and Nick hesitated, scanning the street, then he saw the horse-drawn cab parked a few yards away.

"No! There." A. J. grabbed his arm, pointing the other way. "I'm right behind you."

Nick took off toward the saddled horse tied at the hitching rail. The startled animal reared back against his reins, wall-eyed and snorting at Nick's too-fast approach. Nick jerked the slipknot on the reins and vaulted into the saddle. The horse leaped, then took off at a dead run toward the depot.

Chapter Twelve

Nick abandoned the borrowed horse at the streetcar stables, ducked around parked street cars to stay out of sight, and found a concealed place to wait while he got his bearings of the station's layout. The building was a massive structure with inset windows and doors on all sides and the front access directly under the tall spire of the wooden watch-tower. From what he could tell, it was an ordinary day with travelers moving here and there with nothing disrupting the serene morning. If Tolliver hadn't already gotten to Lainie, or if he wasn't even after her, then she was probably inside the station waiting for the train, and that's what he had to find out. Tolliver's outburst could have ended with the desk clerk, but Nick's gut told him otherwise.

There were too many unknowns and no time to plan. Did Tolliver want just Lainie, or all three of them? Was he planning to kill her? Kidnap her? Did he have an accomplice? Was he taking the train out of town, or did he have a buggy or carriage waiting?

Nick checked the bullets in his revolver, popped out a few bullets from his gun belt, dropped them into his duster pocket, and his fingers brushed against Lainie's note. With a quick glance around, he took the paper out, smoothed out the wrinkles, and read.

Nick,

Please forgive the rather compromising manner in which you found yourself when you awakened. It was by your example that I learned the usefulness of handcuffs as a tool of detainment, so I am sure you will forgive me. It seemed a fitting way to prevent you and A. J. from interfering with what I had to finish. Had I told you of my intent, you would have stopped me, or worse, confronted Ford on my behalf. What I did, I had to do alone in order to put Seaton's death to rest in my heart. I cannot truly be yours while still clinging to the heartache of a memory.

I must also tell you that I cannot bear returning to the place of my birth in the company of lawmen, but since I am a woman of my word, I am turning myself in to Charlotte authorities when I arrive. Your impeccable reputation will therefore remain untarnished. I have much to tell you, and I am sure you have many questions for me, so please don't tarry.

All my love,

Lainie

P.S. While it was thoughtful of you to watch over my derringer, it is so nice to have the pair reunited. A girl just never knows when she may need to use them.

He stuffed her note back into his pocket. She was right. He would have stopped her. With another check of the area, he trotted across the street, joined a family, and moved along with them. The cathedral-ceilinged lobby buzzed with noise and activity of all the people leaving town after the poker tournament and grand ball. Nick moved amongst the travelers, looking over each woman and paying close attention to women and young children, while keeping an eye peeled for Tolliver. Nothing. She wasn't there.

Right then, Nick did his own bit of gambling. Whatever Tolliver wanted with Lainie, and if he hadn't caught her already—which didn't seem likely since there was no evidence an altercation had occurred—then he was waiting somewhere along the boarding platform. The platform was filled with noise, confusion, and distractions—the perfect place to confront Lainie, as well as to aid him in his escape. An incoming train whistle blared shrill and loud over the early morning city, and the crowd began milling toward the boarding area.

Once outside, Nick turned a tight, slow circle, peering into the crowd, searching faces. It seemed every woman was either blonde or carried a child. Too many people. Too much activity. Detraining passengers made the already congested platform even more packed with bodies that moved willy-nilly and seemed to make no progress toward any destination. Needing a vantage point, he spied a stack of shipping crates and climbed up high enough to survey over the heads of the travelers.

Lainie, girl, show me. Where are you?

Then he saw her. In the moment she appeared in an open space, a dark blur of movement rushed her from a recessed doorway. Tolliver grabbed Lainie without a sign of struggle. Nick saw why. Tolliver held a gun on the boy.

Nick jumped down and took off, elbowing his way through the crowd, gaining ground and catching occasional glimpses of Lainie still ahead of him. Tolliver was headed for the far end of the station and, Nick surmised, the getaway transportation he had waiting. With the end of the building mere yards away, Nick had to make a move now or it would be too late. Hugging the station wall for the meager cover it offered, he focused his attention for the shot that would put an end to Tolliver's plans.

Nick yelled, "U. S. Marshal! Everybody down! Out of the way!" He drew his .44 and brought it up to bear. "Tolliver! Let her go!"

People scattered. A path cleared. He took off at a crouching run. A woman screamed.

Tolliver whipped around and swung Lainie in front of him, one arm clamped around her middle, and his gun hand homing in on Nick.

Nick held his shot.

"Muriel! Run!" Lainie screamed. Lainie reared backward, using Tolliver's body as leverage and kicked her feet wildly, throwing him off balance. Twisting out of his grip, she managed a few stumbling steps before she fell, her reticule flying high in the air and coming down far over in the dirt between the tracks.

Tolliver regained solid footing and cracked off a shot at Nick, but it went high, sending people diving for cover. A. J. came around the end of the building, gun drawn, looking for the same clear shot Nick wanted, but also not finding it. Tolliver spun on his heel, his eyes wild with the gleaming frenzy of a trapped animal uncertain from where the next attack would come.

Lainie scrambled up, but her feet caught in her hem, and she tumbled in a tangle of skirts and shoes. With Vance clutched in her arms, Muriel fled toward the protection of a baggage cart when Tolliver swung his gaze and gun upon her. Larnéll whipped past A. J. and, with a reckless leap, threw himself bodily upon Muriel and Vance, taking them to the ground. Vance's terrified, wailing cry made Nick's hair stand on end. A. J. fired. Tolliver might have jerked from the impact or it could have been a faulty step, Nick couldn't tell. A. J. aimed again, but Nick had the clear shot, and his bullet found its mark, although Tolliver only took a few stumbling steps before his return fire burned Nick's thigh, buckling his leg. It saved him from the direct hit of Tolliver's next shot, which tugged his coat sleeve above his elbow.

Lainie darted around Tolliver in her desperate race to reach her child, but Tolliver grabbed her, ramming his gun barrel into her ribs, stopping her struggle as quickly as it began. Nick settled his sights on the middle of Tolliver's broad chest, aching to pull the trigger the instant Lainie was clear.

"Drop your gun, Tolliver. Let her go!"

Tolliver looked toward the end of the building, weighing his chances of getting away, then changed his mind, and started backing toward the tracks, dragging Lainie along with him using her body as a shield. A freight train, two tracks over and on the far side of a parked freight train, headed out of the yard in a slow, chugging speed of steadily increasing momentum.

"I'll kill her! Drop your guns," Tolliver ordered.

"Shoot! Nick, shoot—" Lainie's words choked-off when Tolliver yanked her up and off her feet, swinging her with him in his retreat.

"Turn. Her. Loose." Nick tightened his finger on the trigger.

"Not today, Marshal."

Nick and A. J. moved in as Tolliver lugged Lainie toward the parked train. When he reached the space between the last two train cars, he made a quick glance over his shoulder.

From behind Nick a voice demanded, "Drop your weapons! All of you. Drop your weapons! Release the woman!"

Tolliver fired a shot toward the two police officers closing in on them in the same moment Lainie wrenched free and fell face down on the ground.

"Lainie! Stay there. Stay down!" Nick took fresh aim.

Tolliver fired, and the bullet ricocheted off the station wall. Nick instinctively ducked. If he'd counted right, that was Tolliver's fifth shot, which meant Tolliver probably had one more bullet, but Nick wasn't ruling out a back-up gun.

Tolliver made a running lunge, scooped up Lainie's bag, leaped onto the train car couplings, and jumped down on the other side. Nick followed him over the couplings, ran a few hard-paced yards in pursuit, but his wounded leg wasn't up to the chase, and it gave out, sending him to the dirt. Nick took careful aim at Tolliver's back as the man ran alongside the train. Nick's first shot missed, but the second bullet hit.

Tolliver stumbled, almost went clear down, but somehow not only kept going, but found a burst of strength and speed, leaped, and bellied-down in the open doorway of a passing cattle car, and clambered inside.

Sitting in the doorway with legs dangling, he pulled open the strings on Lainie's reticule, looked inside, then lifted the little bag in one hand and swept off his hat with the other in a wave of victory.

For a few more seconds, Nick watched the train take Tolliver away, then he half-trotted, half-limped around the end of the parked train. When Lainie saw him, she handed Vance back to Muriel and ran to Nick. Running full-out, she threw herself into his arms, nearly taking them to the ground in her relief.

With one arm around her waist, Nick looked past Lainie to A. J. "Where the hell were you? You were supposed to follow me."

A. J. jerked a nod toward the two policemen. "These fine officers seemed confused about whose side I was on, and they suggested I ought to holster my gun until they could figure out who they needed to shoot and who they didn't." He pushed back the front of his hat, grinning. "I introduced us, and we got it figured out. Everyone's happy now."

Nick said, "I need a wire sent out to stop that freight train. There's a man on it named Rutherford Tolliver, and he's suspected of murder. Alert the law on down the line."

"Right away." One of the police officers took off on a run.

A. J. cocked his head as he looked Nick over. "You're getting careless, boy. He got you twice."

Nick glanced down at his bloody trouser leg then at the ragged tear in his coat sleeve. "Yeah, well, if your eyesight was better, you'd have put Tolliver down with your first shot. All you did was graze him."

"Graze him? Hell, I got him just like I planned. You're the one who missed the perfect shot. I could have had a beer drank waiting on you."

Nick grinned. Turning to Larnéll, he said, "Looks like you're braver than you thought."

"I am indeed, Marshal, in more ways than I'd ever thought possible."

"Lainie," Nick said. "Tolliver took your reticule. He looked inside then brandished it like he'd won a trophy. What was in it?"

Lainie raised a stricken gaze to Muriel, her eyes brimming with tears that Nick was surprised to see.

"He took the watch...and one of the derringers."

In those silent moments, Nick saw the loss of hopes and dreams pass between them. Then Muriel's expression softened to show a thoughtful, if not somewhat sad, smile.

"Lainie. You saw the promise you made to Seaton fulfilled. Does it matter so much that Ford has the watch again? Perhaps you're not its keeper. Perhaps the watch has another calling and remaining in your hands is not possible. And the derringer is there to protect it."

Lainie lifted her chin as if defying the logic of Muriel's pragmatic words. "Ford succeeding in taking Seaton's watch again is a bitter failure for me to accept." Her shoulders rose and fell with suppressed sobs that she fought back with deep, shaking breaths, as if refusing to allow disappointment to rule her. "But I—I suppose you're right. It doesn't matter now." She wiped the tears wetting her cheeks, and a little smile showed through. "But you know how I hate to lose."

"You didn't lose, Lainie. Tolliver did. You have me, and you have your son. I'd like the chance to be a father to him," Nick said. "And while we're talking about making plans for the future, I've been meaning to talk to you about something."

"Oh? And what is that?"

"Every time you leave me, I get shot."

Lainie inspected his sleeve and merely frowned at his bloody leg. "What? These little ol' scratches? Why, I believe my derringers have done more damage." She lifted her gaze to meet his, the smirk on her lips as saucy as the gleaming tease in her eyes. "If you could ask Ford, I'm sure he'd agree."

Nick eyed her, opened his mouth to ask, and then clamped it shut on the question. "As a lawman, I don't think I want to know about that. What I do know is, no more guns for you. And while we're discussing this, don't go messing with my handcuffs, and I'll make the coffee from now on, and pour the bourbon." His attempt at a gruff reprimand deteriorated to a grin. "And as for gambling—"

Lainie took hold of the front of his coat and tilted her face up to his. "Be thoughtful of your ultimatums, Marshal, or I just might succumb to a serious case of wanderlust. Southern France is lovely this time of year, and the gambling is magnificent."

Nick drew her closer. "Well, then, let's find us a sky pilot before that wanderlust has a chance to take flight. I'll bet we can agree on a place to settle down and raise a houseful of kids. Didn't you say you still have property in New Orleans?"

"Yes, in fact, I do." Rising on her tiptoes, Lainie pressed a kiss on his lips. "And what do you have to wager on that bet?"

"Just the rest of our lives together, Lainie. Just the rest of our lives."

The End

About Kaye Spencer

Native Coloradoan Kaye Spencer grew up on a cattle ranch in northeastern Colorado. Since 1990, she's lived in a small, rural town located in the heart of the Dust Bowl area of the 1930s in southeastern Colorado. Kaye writes mostly western romances.

Louis L'Amour's western novels, Marty Robbins' gunfighter ballads, and western movies and tv shows inspired her love of the American Old West. Kaye's favorite movie line is from 'Quigley Down Under'. "I said I never had much use for one. Never said I didn't know how to use it." (This is exactly her relationship with her kitchen.)

During Kaye's younger years, she followed the amateur rodeo circuit and experienced life on the thoroughbred racetrack. She even did a stint as a cleaner of sugar beet storage silos (after beets are processed into sugar) to keep down the sugar dust and minimize static electricity in order to avoid an explosion. She soon realized a college education to earn a teaching degree was a safer way to support herself and her three young children.

She earned a B.A. in elementary education which landed her a position as librarian for a 90,000-volume children's library. Her next position was as a teacher of students with special needs. She returned to college for her M. A. in learning disabilities. After several years in the classroom, she worked as a K – 12 principal. She left teaching and public administration for many years to work as a school psychologist and then as the director of exceptional student services for 13 school districts. She ended her career in education as a 6th –12^{th}grades English and history teacher and freshman-level community college teacher.

Kaye is fortunate to spend a lot of time with her family. Many rescued and homeless animals have found a home with her, and more are always welcome. Learn more about Kaye, her books, and where to find her on social media at www.kayespencer.com.

Also by Kaye Spencer

Kaye's Universal Book Link

https://books2read.com/kayespencer

Chicago Lightning

The Dance

Gunfighter's & Ghostriders

Give Me Tomorrow

www.ingramcontent.com/pod-product-compliance
Lightning Source LLC
LaVergne TN
LVHW010918110826
845149LV00013B/2409

* 9 7 9 8 9 9 3 0 8 2 3 2 5 *